Not a Thing to Comfort You

The Iowa Short Fiction Award

Not a Thing to Comfort You

Emily Wortman-Wunder

University of Iowa Press · Iowa City

University of Iowa Press, Iowa City 52242
Copyright © 2019 by Emily Wortman-Wunder
www.uipress.uiowa.edu
Printed in the United States of America
Design by Sara T. Sauers

Printed on acid-free paper

Library of Congress Cataloging-in-Publication Data
Names: Wortman-Wunder, Emily, author.
Title: Not a thing to comfort you / Emily Wortman-Wunder.
Description: Iowa City : University of Iowa Press, [2019] |
Series: The Iowa Short Fiction Award
Identifiers: LCCN 2019011171 (print) |
LCCN 2019017520 (ebook) |
ISBN 978-1-60938-682-5 (ebook) |
ISBN 978-1-60938-681-8 (pbk. : acid-free paper)
Classification: LCC PS3623.O785 (ebook) |
LCC PS3623.O785 A6 2019 (print) |
DDC 813/.6—dc23
LC record available at https://lccn.loc.gov/2019011171

To my parents

Contents

Not a Thing to Comfort You

THE WOMAN CRAWLED into town from the riverbed. Two miles. The elbows of her jean jacket were ripped to shreds and there was tar on her forearms, and gravel, and river mud. That's how it was we knew how far she'd come. That, and the other body, the man's, was found down in the tamarisk, catfish gnawing on his feet. We knew they were together because they each had part of the same animal skull in a pocket: she had the cranial cavity and upper mandible; he had the jaw. I put hers on her nightstand so it'd be the first thing she saw when she woke up.

We wondered among ourselves if his was the name she said sometimes. "Buddy." Hardly a word at all, more of a slur, a sigh, a snarl. We wondered if they were a couple, if this had been done to them together, or if he was the one who'd blacked her eyes. "Or both," sighed Narita. "She got him back, whichever it was," Rebecca said. "Gave him something to think about." The police told us they'd probably been thrown, or thrown themselves, from a train as it sped along the trestle, hugging the water's edge. I gasped, thinking Amtrak, and the other nurses laughed. "No, Annie, these were traineys," said the officer. "You know, train hobos. *Freight* trains."

We washed her hair, lotioned her hands, checked in on her as we hurried past to other patients. Waited for her to wake up.

Sometimes in the evenings I'd think about her, usually as I got ready for bed myself. Standing in the bathroom, scrubbing my whole, rounded teeth with a toothbrush. Whipping the comb through my hair, dark and full along the hairline. Lifting up the sheet and sliding my body in, tired and sore from a long day of honest work. I'd think about how different we were, what different lives we led. I was short and pink and plump with rounded kneecaps, rounded fingertips, a little round belly. My hands could do things, thread an IV, find a vein, sterilize a wound, play Gershwin and Bach on the little upright piano I kept in my dining room.

I wondered if she knew how to do any of this, or what she did do. Her body was long and lean and dry with thinning blond hair that was beginning to grow in where it had been ripped out. Her belly was a bruised flat trapezoid, her belly button square, her kneecaps sharp-edged rectangles. Her forehead was so tall and narrow that sometimes it was all you saw if you popped your head in quick, just glancing over to see if her eyes were open yet; it was the same tawny gray as the rest of her skin, and rough and dry from the weather. Her gums and private parts were swollen and foul with infection. Sometimes her eyeballs raced around beneath their lids, dreaming, and her breath would come in shallow pants. "Shh," Narita would coo if she was there. "Shh, shh, darling. You're with us now."

"Get him, honey," Rebecca would say, one side of her jaw clamped down on a pen as she shook out the IV. "Kick his bu—"

I would shake my hand at them to be quiet, in case she said something else.

Except for the skull, a little piece of rope, and a squashed box of raisins, the kind Narita gave her son to put in his lunchbox, there had been nothing in her pockets. She didn't have money or any sort of driver's license; no nail clippers, no pocketknife, not even a tampon. We told ourselves she must have had a little bag, a backpack, something, and the ones who pushed her off the train had taken it; the detective, one of the days he came in, shrugged. "Sometimes these people don't carry a thing," he said. "That's part of what turns them on to this life."

"Wouldn't that be the life," Rebecca sighed. "No mortgage, no bills. No kids. Nothing to tie you down."

"Nowhere to call home," I corrected. "Not a thing to comfort you."

"*Things*," said Rebecca. "A house can turn around and bite you just as nasty as any old animal. Take a look at Narita's cousin over in Colbrun. Before your time, Annie," she added.

Narita sighed and nodded. "If it hadn't been for that no-good husband of hers, sneaking in at two a.m., they'd all be dead. Came home and there they all were, passed out on the living room floor. The EMTs said if it had been an hour longer they wouldn't of made it."

"Carbon monoxide?" I breathed.

She nodded.

"That's so scary," I said. "I'm going out tonight and getting myself a detector. Isn't that just one too many times you've heard that story?" I let myself take in the whole room with the question, my eyes wide.

"Detectors and deadbolts and moats," Rebecca answered. "All trying to prevent the inevitable. I say when you go, you'll go."

Narita and I shook our heads at her foolishness and, I might add, her total hypocrisy. As if she didn't have smoke alarms and carbon monoxide detectors in the house she and her three boys shared with her fireman fiancé. But this was how we were: Rebecca was the tough, Narita was the good, and I, for some reason, was the little innocent. Only twenty-six, after all. As Rebecca liked to say, squinting at me with something like disapproval, "You've got your whole life ahead of you."

As I walked home I tried to figure out why I'd said what I did. Of course I was a little afraid of carbon monoxide, but no more than any other nurse who's seen a whole family come in limp and blue. It was as though, I justified to myself, the rest of them were so expecting me to say the trembling, wide-eyed thing that it pulled the words right from my lips.

I made my way past the tidy white houses strung along the bluff, each street a little higher than the next. Mine was at the very highest street, overlooking the great river valley and the mountains on either side, with a field of rabbitbrush and sagebrush behind it. I'd bought it when I moved to town two years before, at the tail end of the oil bust, when houses were so cheap it was the same as renting. I'd been able to afford a three-bedroom house on my starting salary, along with furniture and a little red jeep that I used to go four-wheeling and camping. I was still kind of looking for a man to share it all with, even though Ned Flanagan was living with me at the time.

I made for the pasture at the end of the street, the shortcut to my house. My sneakers made hardly any noise in the soft gray dirt, the contours of the pasture following the contour of the bluff, which followed the thick brown snake of the river. I walked out to the far end, where if I stretched my neck a little I could see the spot where they fell from the train. The tracks came so close to the river there they had to be reinforced with beams and steel.

I wasn't interested in how they fell, in the lurch from the floor of the train out into nothingness, the drop, the impact with the rocky river shore that broke her leg, her pelvis, and her teeth.

No. As I peered down at the track, I thought about how they would have seen us: a tidy clump of houses dwarfed by the sagebrush and the hogback hills. A brief scene, in motion, and if they hadn't fallen, soon passed by. I felt a cold lonely feeling as I thought about speeding away, into the unknown, forever leaving, forever being new.

Ned Flanagan and I went to Mattie's Diner that night to eat. We always went to Mattie's on Thursdays, when she oversaw the dinner shift, so we could show how we were supporting her new venture (even if, as Ned would whisper to me later, she put *peas* in the burritos and couldn't make coffee to save her life).

"I've been thinking about your lady," he said when he sat down. "We were out putting in fence posts at that new mansion in the valley. Tedious as hell, and dirty. I mean. Sweat, dust, grease, you name it. Took me two showers to get it off. And your lady, I was thinking, for her it must have been that way all the time. Like coming in from two weeks' hunting, only constantly."

Just for argument's sake, I said, "Maybe that's the price of freedom."

"Hell of a price," he said.

I shook my head and pinched the toe of his boot, up in my lap. For all his faults, Ned sure did have sexy toes. And ankles. All the way up to his head, pretty much.

When Mattie came by, Ned ordered his usual. I was about to order mine when I changed it, at the last minute, to her spicy fish tacos. I've never been a big fan of spicy, or fried fish, or tacos, but there seemed to be something in the air that cried out for change.

After Mattie's we went to the Sagebrush Saloon. We went in and shook off our coats and took our usual spot near the pool table at the far end, where already Hiram Buscay and Jack Armentrout were racking up. I was usually quiet around Ned's pals, but tonight I was quieter than usual and even took a cigarette from Hiram's pack when he offered it around solemnly. The smoke was as harsh as sandpaper in my throat and lungs and my eyes watered so much that Ned in his annoying way came over and put a hand on my shoulder. "You want to go?" he asked in a low voice, but I shook my head.

A song came on the jukebox, "The Six Colors of Mary," that was hot the first summer I moved to the mountains, when I was still making the rounds of the bars and the men and my life seemed to stretch out before me, unknown and mysterious and sure to be exciting. I think the first time I heard it I was sitting on the hood of Ferguson McCall's pickup as he was giving me his little romantic spiel, the one Rebecca, who's gotten it too, called his "darling, won't you fuck me" speech, and at that particular instant—he hadn't laid a finger on me, yet—the excitement and the beauty of life had seemed almost unbearable. So when that song came on the jukebox I just had to get up off my stool and dance, alone, my face turned up to the dark and smoky ceiling and my hands wrapped around my elbows. Ned watched me with a look that said, there's my crazy girlfriend, isn't she sweet?

That night I ran myself a bath, deep and clean as forgetting; when I got out Ned had fallen asleep. I poured myself a drink and sat by the open window and watched the lights of the town and of the river and of the stars above. And I thought: chair, glass, rum. She had none of this. And I imagined, undoing my robe, the men in town looking up here at me, faintly lit by the town lights, my rounded belly, my rounded breasts, my plump little thighs, up here looking down on the town like a goddess. Or a whore. *She'd* know this feeling, I thought. She'd understand how sometimes comfort is not enough.

Rebecca called the next morning to tell me the woman had woken up. "She says her name is Nancy," she announced over the phone.

"Nancy Higgins," the woman agreed when I'd gotten in and was disengaging her IV.

The detective had already been in and had gotten his first statement, Rebecca said to me. She tried to listen in at the door but then Nancy told her everything anyway. Everything there was to tell, which wasn't much. She only remembered a little: the threats, the fight. Being pushed. The dead man was her boyfriend—"my man," she called him. His name wasn't Buddy but we'd already formed a silent agreement not to ask about that. His name was Christopher Karst.

"Christopher Cursed?" asked Rebecca, her eyebrows flaring.

"Karst," said the woman in her careful gravelly voice. "Karst. Some kind of rock." She shaped a rock layer with her hand above the bedsheet, only the gesture was too much for her and her hand sank down, weary.

Of course we were curious and asked all sorts of things, where she was from, how long she'd been riding the trains, what her life had been like before and during and what she was going to do now.

Not too many of our questions got answered. She'd start, fair enough, but she'd start at the beginning of the story where none of us could make head or tail of anything and long before she got to any of the specifics she'd have waved her hand, wearily, and let it fall as her tongue lapsed into silence. "Where are you from?" was answered by a story that began with her riding a motorcycle up into the deep green hills, her knees cinched tight around some man who wasn't Karst and wasn't Buddy (we didn't think) and maybe wasn't a real man at all but just some idea of what a man should be.

"I know that man," Rebecca said later, over lunch, when we three were hogging the table under the window. "That man's *not* my ex-husband, by way of example. But he could be Fergie McCall." I laughed, partly at the way her eyebrows looked like they were going to leap off her face and partly because it was true: that's how Ferguson was, an idea of a man. And he had made me, I realized at that moment, feel like an idea of a woman. Was that what I wanted?

"That man is my man," said Narita, smiling one of her gentlest smiles with just a hint of lust buried within it.

Rebecca chimed in obediently that of course her Bill was that man too, and they all looked at me to see what I was going to say about Ned and I just had to shake my head. "Nope," I said. "Absolutely not."

"Come on," Rebecca said, stabbing her salad. "He's sweet, right?"

"Sweet and bland," I said. "Like he could go the rest of his life with his boots under the bed and my bra on the back of the door until we both drop over dead. You know? He just has no concept of ambition."

"Oh," said Rebecca meaningfully. "You want Dr. *Rosario*."

Dr. Rosario. We all three closed our eyes for a minute to conjure him, so young, with his new baby, and that ravishing way he had of suddenly leaping up and blushing when his wife called, or when one of us stood just a shade too close. Then we brushed the crumbs off our scrubs, already feeling wanton in comparison.

No, I thought as I went about my rounds, swabbing anuses and poking fingers, Dr. Rosario was not what I wanted either. Ned as a doctor would still be Ned, only we'd have our perfect green lawn and our flotilla of soccer champs and spelling bee winners instead of a house in need of paint and a new porch.

I went by Nancy's room when I had a few minutes; I was sort of hoping she'd be asleep. I just wanted to watch her. But she was awake, and when she caught sight of me she did a sort of fish-like wiggle that seemed to be a gallant attempt to sit up. "Good morning, then," she said in her gravelly voice. "Or it must be good afternoon now. It's so hard to tell sometimes."

I showed her the push button on her bed frame again, up arrow for up, down arrow for down. "Buttons," she said. "I've never been one for buttons."

I laughed, and took her temperature, took her blood pressure, all things the aides usually do, and probably had done, just a few minutes before.

"Another sunny day. Seems like that's about all there is here," she said to me, and I wondered if she meant this as an opening. Wondered if I should take it: What are you used to? I could say, casually.

Instead I said, leaning forward to barely touch the little animal skull still sitting on her nightstand, "I put this here for you. I didn't know if you'd want it."

She smiled one of her long thin smiles and said, "How sweet." And then nothing for a long time and we both stared out at the blindingly blue sky and I was beginning to resign myself to making do with "how sweet," when she continued, "That Karst. 'I got the part that bites,' he said, 'and you got the part that dreams.' That's what he said." She shook her head. "So much folderol, to me."

"You don't go for folderol?" I asked, casually, pretending to mark something on her chart. I felt suddenly flooded with an odd, dangerous hope: maybe that was what made her what she was. Something so easy as not caring for the little things.

"Some of us can do with less, you know?" was all she said, smiling a lopsided grin that made her nose and chin come forward into sharpened points.

I nodded, breathless, hoping for the more that never came.

After that I stopped in whenever I got a chance. I don't know why. She rarely said much to me and I didn't know how to ask her about things the way Rebecca and even Narita could; yet when they were there I'd make my excuses and leave. All they ever asked about was her childhood, her sex life, the times she tried to go straight. I no longer wanted to hear what loose, rambling confessions they elicited and once or twice I almost said to Nancy, when we were alone, "It's not like you have to answer them. You could just say no, I don't choose to talk about that."

But I never did. When I was in her room—picking up little bits of trash from the floor, straightening the stuff on her gift shelf, the flowers and teddy bears the other nurses brought in out of pity—I mostly held my breath and listened. Sometimes I tried to get her to talk by complaining about my life, about Ned, or the house, or how I was on call so much it seemed like I could hardly get away. She'd laugh, a single braying syllable that was never spontaneous—"*Haw!*"—and I'd feel gratified. Even blush a little. "Yeah, I know," I'd answer, "can you believe that's what he *said*?"

Of course Rebecca picked up on it. "How's your girlfriend doing?"

she'd say when she passed me sneaking back up to my floor after a quick detour. Or once, when she caught me in Nancy's room: "This little nurse has quite a crush on you, Ms. Higgins. Don't let it go to your head."

"*Haw!*" Nancy laughed, the same as if it had been one of my carefully crafted stories.

Narita was trying to be nice to me, I think, when she cornered me in the second-floor station one day and pressed a stack of pamphlets into my hand. "Just make sure she knows about what's available to her. Especially the free dental clinic. We can even sign her up. They could do bridgework on those—" she broke off, pressing her fingers into the lips that covered her own strong teeth.

The pamphlets. I flipped through them, shuddering, as I made my way to Nancy's room. Local social services, the employment agency, the food bank. Just the thought of telling her about these things made me want to stutter and blush. I tucked them into my scrubs pocket as I knocked on the open door.

Nancy was in one of her black moods. I couldn't get so much as a snort out of her and she sat and stared at the end of the bed as if she were alone. I thought about how soon, perhaps as soon as next week, she'd be on the outside again. Free to come into our homes. Free to jump on a train and leave us all behind. I tried to check the dosage on her antibiotic IV but my hands were shaking too much to read it.

"So I guess you've heard," I said finally. "They're going to be letting you out of this joint at last."

I dropped the roll of tape I was using to reset her tubes. She snorted derisively.

"About time, huh?" I added. "Be nice to have your freedom back?"

I was stretching to adjust the light above her bed when she said, in a voice I'd never heard before, "It ain't like what you think it is, you know, the rolling life. It ain't pretty. It ain't cute."

As if I'd ever favored a cute thing in my life. She'd fallen for Rebecca and Narita's version of me as if that was all there was. But I kept my cool; said, stomach cringing, "There's more to life than cute and pretty."

She expelled her breath in one long stream and refused to look at me. I couldn't have told you anything I wanted more that minute than to have her answer me; I thought I'd go crazy with it. She kept her silence.

I knelt by the bed. "Nancy," I said, almost reaching for her hand. "Tell me what it was like. Please. Tell me one of your stories."

She rolled her eyes, but I could tell I was getting to her.

"I won't judge you, you know. Not like the others," I said.

Still without looking at me, she began. "I'd been riding the rails about two or three years, on-again, off-again. I came through a town I'd been through plenty before, even been locked up there once. Wouldn't have got off again except I hadn't eaten for two, three days, and I knew there was a place in town that always had good leavings.

"But these kids got in my way. Gave me shit the way kids do. Tagging along. Menacing. Then we passed a sandwich someone had dropped. All wrapped up, perfectly clean, had my name on it. Only they saw how much I wanted it. Held it out of my way. Stepped on it and everything else. I won't go into the details except to say by the time I scraped it off the street it was only a memory of a sandwich, wet and what-else. I ate it though. Had to.

"But this was how I got to eat it at all. They weren't going to leave me a thing, I could see that. Weren't going to let me go about my business. So I did what I had to do. You get me? What I had to do. Not a regret in the world."

I nodded, almost taking her hand again. I couldn't think of a thing to say. There was no question of giving the pamphlets to her now, so I chucked them onto her bed and fled. As I hurried away, her voice burned in my head. "I did what I had to do. You get me?" It kept me awake all that night and part of the next: What did she do? Would I have been able to do the same? How do you know when you're so far into a corner that only that, whatever it is, will work?

· · ·

It was Rebecca's idea to put together a collection for Nancy, a bag of necessities and clothes and a couple hundred dollars in cash. We even put a phone card in there and started asking around about cheap rentals. Ned got into it too and went so far as to round up someone's old Buick clunker, a heap of blue metal that barely ran but that he drove up to the hospital like the elf chosen to deliver Santa's bounty. "Lookit," he said. "Two hundred and fifty-eight thousand miles and she still runs as reliable as taxes. Wouldn't think it possible for an American car, would you?"

"Oh for Pete's sake," I said crossly. It was my break and he was using up precious minutes of my time. "What are we supposed to do with this? I don't even know if she knows how to drive."

What I should have said was, I don't even know if she knows how to register a car. In all the stories I'd heard from her there hadn't been a lot of mundane details about living the kind of boring, rule-driven life the rest of us led. Did she know how to vacuum? How to buy peanut butter? Ned shrugged and grinned. "Anything I can do to put her on the right path," he said, and I had to bite my tongue to prevent an argument.

As it turned out the hospital lawyers wouldn't let us do anything with the car. Rebecca suggested finally that we leave it with Ned—i.e., in my driveway—until we had a better sense of what Nancy wanted to do. Rebecca said all this in that self-important hushed voice that made me feel like an eight-year-old, so I asked spitefully if she really meant until we found out whether Nancy was going to turn into a responsible citizen or if she would bail on all of us and skip town like the hobo she was. The other two just looked at me as if I'd made a dirty joke in church and by the time I left work I almost wanted to cry.

When I got home I sat in the dark and pictured myself riding a box-car out of town, holding onto the edge of an open door the way people in the city hold the poles along the aisle of a bus. For some reason I pictured myself in a long jeans skirt, my sheepskin coat, and brown nylon snow boots, my cute curly hair washed and combed. About as much like a trainey as someone in a $500 pop-up tent is like a homeless person.

That settles it, I thought. I'm stuck here. I laid my head down on our sticky tablecloth and let the tears come.

The next evening I filled in for one of the night nurse's shifts. Passing Nancy's room on the way to my wing, I heard the hiccupping sounds of someone sobbing and the harsh rasp of someone else's whisper, steady and insistent. I paused on my silent-soled shoes and bent my head to the open door.

"I can't do it. I can't go back there. I can't do it," came someone's whining, mewling, snot-wet voice. Deformed that way, it could have been anyone's.

"You don't have to," came the other person's voice. "We're here to help. You're going to make it just fine." The voice, a woman's, was calm, sensible, understanding. Except for this it sounded like the pitch and timbre of Rebecca's. I leaned in closer.

"They'll kill me this time, I know they will. And it's winter coming on soon."

"That's why we've gone out and done this for you."

"Charity. I was raised never to take it—"

"Not charity, honey, a helping hand. Like opening a door. To get you back on your feet. You've had so much taken from you."

"I know it, I know it. Oh, you all are so good to me. And I don't deserve it, I don't."

"Never say that."

I felt something like nausea in the pit of my stomach, and I don't know what caused it more, hearing Nancy reduced that way, groveling and desperate, or the way Rebecca was so infinitely sympathetic and responsible, so grown-up. So unlike me, just chucking the pamphlets on the bed and running away. I hated her then the way I'd never hated anyone before or since; the worst of it was how I knew it was all show, all fakery. Rebecca was no more sympathetic or understanding than I, yet there she was, pretending to be the voice of reason, and Nancy was eating it up. I stumbled away, determined to outdo Rebecca at her own game.

That night I was a veritable angel of goodness and responsibility. I cajoled Mrs. Humphrey into taking her medications orally. I made little Billy Gutierrez, recovering after another asthma attack, laugh as I administered his injections. On my break I went and bought a candy bar and put it in my pocket, to bring to Nancy at the end of my shift.

My shift ended at eight a.m., and out the window I could see the town revving up their cars, getting ready to go into work. The sunlight was bright and brittle, and I had second thoughts as I went down the hall with a Snickers bar in my pocket. How responsible is it to bring a patient with nutritional problems a candy bar at eight in the morning? I stopped in at the cafeteria and picked up an orange, the only kind of fruit there that didn't look like someone had used it to play soccer.

I went in, prepared to be cheerful, yet firm. Here's a Snickers for you, I imagined saying, but eat the orange first. To my surprise, the detective was there, and Narita, and the hospital administrator. Nancy was sitting up on the bed in someone's approximation of street clothes, filling out her release forms. Her handwriting was spidery and excruciatingly slow and she kept chuckling at her own incompetence as she went, while everyone else stood around her trying to hide their impatience.

They were all thrilled to see me, of course—how convenient! Annie can be her taxi!—and I made a good show of being thrilled that Nancy was finally going to get out, to be on her own. "You scared?" I said, just to make conversation, and Narita gave me a look.

Nancy took my question seriously, though. "Naw," she said. "Be nice to get out to where someone isn't waiting on me hand and foot every two minutes. Be on my ownsome again."

We got her all checked out, set up the payment plan, got the Medicaid paperwork completed. Narita carried the bag we'd packed for her out to my car and even the detective and the administrator went with us to the lobby, shook her hand, gave her their cards, which she kept holding as we went out to my car, like they were tickets to a show.

· · ·

Before I started up the jeep I had to lean over and untwist her seat belt and plug it in. At the same time, I straightened the collar of the beige work shirt someone had put on her, and she let me, the way a dog might let you clip its leash on. Sitting in the front seat of my car, she seemed thinner and faded, and not so tall; she had a way of lifting her chin and squinting out into the world like it was all just too bright for her. I handed over the orange and the Snickers and gave her my little rehearsed line. It didn't seem like she wanted to eat at all but she obediently started peeling the orange, the pungent oil spurting into the space between us. I had a sudden sense of being unable to take a deep breath, as if the air in my jeep was low in oxygen.

I said, "So you really want to do this?" I meant it as a joke, but she didn't laugh.

I drove her across town to the dark little basement studio Rebecca had sweet-talked the owner into renting for practically nothing, furnished. I helped her unlock the front door, found the light switches, showed her the cabinets full of mismatched pans and dishes. I showed her the telephone with its list of all our numbers and the calendar that already had the dates for her dental work marked on it. I carried her suitcase over to the bed, put the valise with her personal effects and her medications on the bureau. She stood by the door and watched me.

"Well," I said. "This is nice, isn't it? All this space, all to yourself." I started putting away the groceries Rebecca had bought and left on the counter. And then, to buck her up, I added, "Dragged yourself into town by your elbows and now look at you, practically an honest citizen."

She grunted, stumping across to the window on her reinforced leg cast. Her chin was on a level with the windowsill and her nose poked out at the blades of grass.

"Like living six feet under," I joked. "In more ways than one."

Her face didn't change, just kind of sank into itself, like someone was letting the air out of it. "Be nice to be a regular folk for a bit," she said. Like she was expecting I wanted to hear that, I thought. I wanted to tell her that I wasn't Rebecca or Narita. That she could be herself with me. Maybe, if I'd said that, things would have turned out differently.

Instead I said, "Course, they want to make you think they're saving your life."

"Maybe they are," she answered, in a pious voice that turned my stomach. She limped across the room to the bathroom, wincing occasionally. Like a lion measuring the width of its cage. She flipped on the bathroom light, flipped it off, flipped it back on. I kept putting away her groceries, wiping down the mouse-turdy shelves with a shredding piece of paper towel. I could sense we were on the brink of falling into the same ways we'd had in the hospital. Here we were in a new place, and I wanted to do more, reach out, dig in, do something that would be forbidden when we were surrounded by everybody else. I paused, scraping at an old crust of something with my fingernail, before saying, "You know. Rebecca and the rest of them. The do-gooders. You're their project now, you know that. Their little way to show the world, look at me, I'm such a saint." The anger I'd felt in the middle of the night was starting to boil up. "It's all totally fake."

"Puts the roof over my head," she said, half turning my way.

"It's *totally fake*. They do it to prove something about themselves. It's not about compassion. It's not about caring for who you really are." She still looked unconvinced, and, desperate, I hit on the thing to make her listen. "Take this. What Rebecca said to me this morning. Bragging. She said, 'I have that woman eating out of the palm of my hand. I have her begging me.'" The lies burned my tongue, lit me up from within.

"I never beg."

"I'm just saying what she said. 'She was groveling all over,' Rebecca told me. I stood up for you. I said, 'Not Nancy. No way.' But Rebecca wouldn't let up. Came up with all sorts of lies. Even said you'd said that you didn't deserve this. Said you begged her not to make you go back. I just shook my head. But you see the kind of people you're dealing with here."

Nancy didn't answer, just stumped over to the window again. I guess I hardly expected her to know what to say. But the silence was like fire.

"I just say it like I see it," I said finally, snapping out the empty grocery bag and folding over the top edge to make a liner for the trash can. "All I say is, you better hold onto that skull of yours, the one your friend said was for dreaming. Cause dreams is all you got, now, same as the rest of us."

I don't know what I expected to happen. I had hopes, of course. A strange new presence in my third bedroom, maybe. Or at least the phone calls, from places like Kansas City, Denver, Santa Fe, links to a life somewhere else.

What I didn't expect was Narita's scream when we opened the door the next day—we just knocked and let ourselves in, as if it were still the hospital—the bureau open and emptied, the kitchen cabinets, the fridge. Nancy even managed to take the landlord's TV.

In the first gasp I thought she had been kidnapped, dragged back into her nefarious past by forces too dark to imagine. Then Narita said, in a tone I'd never heard her use before, "Well, I guess *pink* was not her style." And she held up the shirts Nancy had left behind, and the stockings, and the pants. Narita's own castoffs, most of them. And my polka-dotted top. I'd pictured her posing in it, jaunty and campy, when I'd pulled it out of my closet; pictured her leaning in and whispering the secret identity of Buddy, telling it to me and no one else. Was it for this I'd told my lies?

But it was the note that felt like a kick in the teeth. On the stovetop, where we wouldn't see it right away but couldn't miss it: "For Anny," was all it said, and weighting it down was the top half of the rodent skull. I took it up with numb fingers, that grayish knobby bone focusing something in my own brain. A throb, a thrum. The folderol was what she left for me; the folderol that was my lot all along. I swept the skull to the floor and stepped on it, trembling.

Gustav and Vera

HELOISE PULLS UP in front of my house the morning after the recital, crushing a few tulips with the passenger-side wheels of her Honda. I sigh ever so faintly and put down the biography of Mozart I've been reading. She's come, I'm sure, to talk about last night's recital; Vera Ludenya, the famous violinist, and our Gustav on piano, together again, together for the last time. There will be the sniffing about how Gustav flubbed the fast notes and Vera was cold in the adagios; Heloise can't play a note but she can gripe with the best of them. Heloise is Gustav's third wife, the oldest living one, and I notice that this morning she is showing her age. Her eyes dart back and forth as she comes up the walk, and she's digging in her purse like she needs a cigarette and she needs it now.

I bring out the sweet rolls and make a pot of coffee. She strides through the house with her head up, looking like a Parisian model—a Parisian model in her sixties, of course. She has on a skirt and jacket ensemble that can pass, in Bluff, Nebraska, for a tailored suit, and there's a gauzy scarf tied around her throat. As usual I feel like a plain Jane beside her. I call the music library over at the college, and let them know I won't be in until noon. I've been emeritus since I turned sixty, so it hardly matters. You might not believe it to look at us, but Heloise is my closest friend. She's also the nearest thing I have to family anymore—does having been married to the same man count as a family relation? I was Maestro Gustav Behr's second wife, in what I've heard him call the icebox marriage.

I wipe down the vinyl slats of the deck chairs and lay out my grandmother's bone china. Heloise sits in a deck chair and smokes while she watches me work.

"Well, Meardis, he's done it this time," she says. "Number Four ought to kick him out. She really ought to."

I smile and roll my eyes, delicately. I don't even ask why she says this; Heloise has been seeing Martha's demise for thirteen years.

Martha is a good twenty years younger than either of us. She has two distinctions, besides being the youngest wife: at twelve years, her marriage to Gustav has been the second longest yet; and it looks likely, by all accounts, to be the last. It's also the only one besides the first to have produced a child—which has made Heloise and me look a little like odd blips between two real marriages. I've always thought this was part of Heloise's grudge against her. After the obvious things, like the affair.

"You should have seen her," Heloise says. "She was wearing this purple thing—a monstrosity."

"I love that one," I say. "It makes me think of gardenias." I like Martha, although she is cautious around me.

"Honestly, Meardis. Gardenias don't come in purple." The plucked line of her eyebrows kinks with annoyance but the venom has gone out of her voice and I smile to myself as I pick a piece of sugary walnut off the table and put it on my plate. This is my role, you see. I keep the peace. Just last week Gustav, emeritus too, said as much as he popped out of my office. "Keeping me in line, eh, Meary?" he said, winking. "You keep us all in line." I was holding him to his promise to help me update our Paganini collection, and he was trying to skip out of it. Five years now he's been putting it off; I let him go this time because in a few days he'll have all the time in the world, once his symphony responsibilities are done.

Heloise is telling me the details of the recital, the Mozart sonata they played first, the Brahms, the Poulenc. Ah, the Poulenc, I think, nodding. That's the one I suggested myself; Gustav had been leaning toward Shostakovich, much too dark. The Bluff audience might actually have to listen to that one, and I've been to enough guest artist recitals to know how little listening gets done. I now prefer to wait for the symphony concert.

Vera's looking old, Heloise continues, positively elderly. I suppose that would be true; Vera Ludenya is one of Gustav's oldest friends. They used to play chamber music when they were at Julliard, had a piano trio with the famous cellist Arnold Eggston, and a piano quintet, too, for a while. She was sort of an adjunct figure in all our marriages, in her dove-colored raincoats and her fixed smile; we've all poured her morning coffee. She's a refugee, like Gustav, from the fallen aristocracy of classical music. It was one of Heloise's rare moments of brilliance to suggest to the orchestra manager that they bring her in as the soloist for Gustav's final concert as the conductor of the Bluff Philharmonic. Gustav has talked of nothing else since it seems. The past month he has been giddy to the point of foolishness as he putters about the music building.

"But the big news of the evening came after the Poulenc," Heloise says.

"The news?"

Heloise looks carefully at me. "They're going on the road, to play sonatas. A post-retirement tour. Gustav's idea, but Vera was dreadfully enthusiastic. And afterward there's talk of an artist-in-residency at Eastman, where Vera teaches."

A huge splash of coffee falls out of my cup into my lap. I rub at the stain with a napkin, which makes my thigh jiggle, but the stain only gets larger and smearier. This couldn't be Gustav's idea, I think, stupidly. What about the Paganini collection?

She taps her ash into a saucer.

She thought they were up to something the way Gustav kept grinning and piano-noodling between pieces, but it wasn't until after the last applause died out and Gustav stood up from behind the piano and cleared his throat that she knew. It was at this time, Heloise says, that she began to watch Martha. Now, had I been there, I would have been watching Gustav: the way he took Vera's hand—was it cupped in his own, like a rare butterfly, or half-grabbed from the side, the way he takes every soloist's hand after a concert?—whether his smile started from his eyes, or whether it began from his nose and smoothed out, superciliously, toward his ears. I would have been sensitive to the nuances in his voice, to see if this were something he really wanted, and had been hiding all this time from Martha, from his colleagues, from me. Heloise, however, paid attention only to Martha.

"She didn't see *this* coming, I could tell," Heloise says. "Her mouth just opened and shut, opened and shut. Then she started taking these little tiny breaths in—none out, just in—and she swelled up like a big purple whale. I thought she was going to have a medical emergency any minute. It was wonderful."

I get up to find an ashtray. The table joggles as I stand and Heloise glances at me, a stream of smoke coming from her nostrils.

I scrub my skirt with a wet washcloth first, surrounded by my kitchen, my home. The marbled linoleum, the cut tulips in a vase on the counter, the framed prints of foreign cities I've never visited; always too busy, with the library, with one project or another for Gustav. To one side the sliding glass doors with their view of the garden and the lake; to the other side the piano, the shelves of books. Bounded on every side, but snug.

I suppose I fell in love with the musician's life that Gustav described, his head heavy and scented against my chest—the bittersweet golden evenings, the post-concert receptions with the leading soloists of the day, the smoky sight-reading sessions in the apartments of exiled European musicians, who somehow carried with them the atmosphere of Vienna and Paris. "Meary. From me to my teacher is an invisible connection, and from him to all the great pianists of our time; he was taught by Franz Liszt, who also taught Rachmaninoff: the invisible golden string. You could trace the line all the way back to Beethoven, I'd bet you, all the way back to Mozart." When I hear Gustav whistling Mendelssohn in his emeritus office down the hall, when he drops by to ask me to order an essential recording or set of parts for the library, that golden string shimmers along my shoulders too. The Paganini collection? An extension of the string.

I rummage through the pantry shelves, looking for the ashtray. The damp spot keeps brushing clammily against my leg. What about Lisa, Gustav's ten-year-old daughter—he'll just drag her off? And Martha's mother, in a home over near White Falls—what about her? I start to get worked up. It'll be like the way we had to sell my mother's farm, the way he took the piano when he moved out; the way he does everything. I make myself take a deep breath. Bygones.

I put the ashtray under the end of Heloise's cigarette. It's her second; the stub of the first is off in the grass somewhere, or perhaps in the lake.

"Really, they've both been wanting this for a long time. Gustav has always felt shackled to the Philharmonic and the college—you knew that, right? How could you not?" Without losing her smugness, Heloise has opened her eyes very wide and a saccharine note has crept into her voice.

"But the Philharmonic is his baby," I say. I am remembering Gustav with black hair, standing in the middle of the music library, shouting, "All I want is a complete set of scores for Beethoven's symphonies! How can you not have this? What sort of godforsaken speck on the map is this?" I was twenty-two years old, and he made me cry. Not because of the yelling but because I realized, at that moment, that Bluff, Nebraska, had a true musician in it, and that we were unworthy. I wonder spitefully if Heloise has any idea of what being a true musician means, but then I make myself stop. Heloise cannot help herself.

We've stopped talking and Heloise has lit a third cigarette. She looks out over my lawn, at my carefully tended flower beds and vegetable gardens—she lives in a condominium with a grounds crew, and keeps plastic plants. The silence that falls as we look off, away from each other, is a familiar one.

When Heloise leaves I get my gardening gloves and dandelion prong and go out to weed the tulips. "Meardis Behr," I tell myself, "You are not going to second-guess Heloise."

I say this out loud, for better effect, but I answer myself internally.

I'm not second-guessing, I say to myself. I'm just being cautious.

I try not to suspect things. Particularly I try not to suspect that Heloise has done this on purpose.

Baby dandelions and the insistent shoots of bindweed have sprung up all through the flower beds. I stab the double teeth of the weeding prong into the soil and push it down along the length of those persistent roots.

When Heloise first called me, in the early bitter days after their divorce, I was surprised that after all, I didn't hate her. I thought I would; she had been my Martha, the stone in my marriage that I could feel but couldn't see. But she was so nervous. She laughed loudly and too much, and she kept saying, "You must think I'm such a jerk, a real jerk." The rings on her fingers knocked percussively against the phone and twice, during the long conversation, she dropped the receiver. I listened, and felt a calmness spreading through me, replacing the feelings I'd had for her before. It made me giddy. Here was the enemy, and she was mine. "Why would I think you're a jerk?" I answered, my voice like strawberry ice cream.

You see, this is how I am: I have coffee with Heloise, tea with Martha, and the stepchildren send me Christmas cards. Lisa stays with me when her parents go out of town. I can kiss them all goodbye, step out on the deck, take in the deep cold smell of the lake and the sadness, beneath, of the prairie. I can go down to my flowerbeds and work; a breeze scuds now across the lake and fluffs the nape of my neck. Of course I ache some nights, sick of loneliness. But I don't mind.

For what is a wife, really? Someone who remembers the children, makes hors d'oeuvres, entertains the guests. These were never my skills. I am more like a Tonto, someone who understands the instructions before they've been given. I know things: I know that the cough before the name of a piece—as in "Berlioz's, ahem, *Symphonie Fantastique*"—means that the work is standard, but not earth-shaking: it is enough to have a recording or two and the score on file. But a cough *after*—well, that means I should buy all the recordings the library can afford. Through Gustav, I have made the Bluff State College music library the third-best in the state; it's been a long and fruitful collaboration. That's something I can stand on.

But Heloise has done something; she's gone behind my back and meddled. Thanks to you, I say to her in my mind, Gustav will walk out of this town like it was just another phase in his life. I stab and rip. Grass runners pull out in strips.

That woman. She has never been able to accept things and not meddle. It is like her hair, which she has cut short and dyed. Bright and snappy, like her. I have let mine go gray, and I wear it longer than a woman with faded hair should. I am content, you see, with things as they are. I have my garden, my bathtub, my job: I don't need the blood and heat of family life, or the frenetic ecstasy of sex.

The wet grass chills me and another buffeting wind from the lake splits my hair in two, like fingers, and pushes me forward so that I feel the binding of my underclothes. I'm hit by a longing so intense and unexpected that it leaves me gasping.

The phone rings and I rush to answer it, certain it is Martha, needing advice, or perhaps even Gustav, but it is only Heloise, asking if

I have found her scarf. "I don't believe so," I say, my heart pounding and flooding me with blood. So hurried that I've gotten mud all over the receiver. When has Martha ever called me for advice, I ask myself scornfully. When she wanted to know what fertilizer to put on the roses to improve their bloom?

The next day I find myself at the guest artist brunch. We are sitting in folding chairs, facing the table of honor, which is the only table, so I am trying to balance a china plate on my lap while I eat a slice of melon. Heloise sits beside me, whispering. I do not have to hear every word she says to know what she is saying, because we are looking at Vera, Gustav, Martha, and Lisa, spread out in a line at the table of honor. Lisa catches my eye and waves, a little four-fingered curl. I ought to just follow them to New York, I think, smiling at my imagined temerity.

Gustav is just beyond earshot, laughing a little from time to time. He's wearing a white turtleneck that brings out the ruddy color of his face but makes his amazingly still-thick white hair seem a little yellowed. He looks relaxed and happy, leaning first to one side and then to the other to whisper in his wife's ear or in Vera's. I am giving in to resignation. How could someone like him ever be content with retirement? He will have his way, like he always does.

Vera is distinctly older. This is the first thing that I notice. Her hair has turned completely silver, although her eyebrows are as black as ever. "Dye," says Heloise. I think this is what she says, because it would make no sense for her to say "Die."

Although she is not making total sense this morning. I sense she feels victory slipping, plus she is beginning to regret her offer to serve as Vera's chauffeur. She's had to drive Vera to the florist's, the grocery, the bookstore, the Thursday-night recital, the master classes yesterday, the brunch today, and the concert tonight. "She's got her nose in every pocket in Bluff," Heloise said when she met me in the lobby before brunch.

Vera looks a little evasive. She is smiling as she talks to Gustav, but there is a strained quality to her smile. She almost seems as though she's watching the door. Her wrists rest delicately on the linen tablecloth, one on either side of her plate, but every so often her arms tense, as if she's bracing herself.

"Martha looks like a defensive end in that dress," whispers Heloise to me.

I am not sure what a defensive end is, but I nod. Martha does have an air of defensiveness about her. Her mascara is a little smudged and she alternately stares straight in front of her or at the side of Gustav's head. She's shredding a breakfast roll on her plate into tiny fragments. From my distance I can still feel her simplicity, her vast generosity. At the same time she seems more vulnerable than ever; she lets her eyes rest upon the audience and I imagine she is looking for me. I sense opportunities opening, precarious, and it makes me restless.

"And Gustav," Heloise continues.

And Gustav. For the first time since our divorce I have been visited with imaginings: what will it be like when he is gone?

"That white turtleneck! Do you suppose he picked that out himself, or does Martha dress him now?" Heloise chews furiously between whispers.

The brunch's speaking events are about to begin. It is going to be a tribute to Gustav. Several of the older women in the audience—Friends of the Philharmonic members, or orchestra players from the early days—have little packets of Kleenex out. Martha has hers, I notice, but Vera has none. I think I see her swallow a yawn.

It's after the president of the Friends of the Philharmonic takes the podium that Vera gets up. The president is deep into her tribute to Gustav, so I am not sure that anyone notices Vera. Heloise and I notice, and Heloise elbows me.

"Go talk with her," she whispers.

I would rather watch Gustav.

"*I* can't go," she says. "I've been working on her all weekend. Just go."

Vera isn't in the ladies' room. She's on the phone, facing away from me. Her voice has changed, no longer the clipped, well-postured syllables that I remember, but something deep and desperate. I want to go back but I don't. I sit down on a bench, far enough away that I can't really hear her conversation, and wait. I look down at the floor so that I don't seem to be eavesdropping. I can't hear much of it. Just pieces:

"—forsaken little town. They—"

I blush, for Bluff's sake, and bite my lip.

"They want me to *sign*. Sign. What should—"

"—so pathetic, so old. It breaks my heart. To think of what he used to be, remember? Those recitals he gave at Julliard—"

I blush again. Gustav? Old? Can't she see the charm he has still? The way the corners of his eyes crease before he smiles, the way in the instant between the crease and the smile you're held, wondering, waiting to see if he'll smile again?

"—such high hopes when I came here. I don't know. I don't know what I was thinking. But he sounded so *vigorous* on the telephone! All that talk—"

My lips are suddenly dry. I look in my purse for some chapstick.

"But what do I do? What should I do? I *can't* hurt him. There's got to be some way to sign and then get out—"

"All right. All right then," she says, and replaces the receiver. She paces away from me down the hall, clenching and unclenching her hands. When she turns around she stops, seeing me.

"I'm just waiting for the phone," I say, twitching my lips against the chapstick. But I don't get up.

"Meardis," she says after a moment, as if I've taken her breath away.

I am surprised and pleased that she remembers my name. I am the type that people like her usually forget.

Maybe this is why I wait. I look at the floor again, and put away my chapstick. I don't look up until she speaks to me.

"It's not that I don't adore Gustav, dear. It's not that I don't respect him. But I must be absolutely frank about the quality of his playing. For me, the music must come first."

I nod, my cheeks stinging from this dismissal of Gustav. Her voice has become brisk and impeccable again, and she folds her hands together.

"Although I find this very compelling. To walk out before that audience, the glitter, the darkness—I am certain I will never get enough of performing."

I nod some more. Her black eyes center themselves on me.

"Not too many young musicians want to be paired with—someone mature. And no one our age cares for the demands of touring. Only Gustav..." Her voice lingers on his name and it makes me want, like a four-year-old, to snatch the name back. She continues, "If I could only be certain he would prepare? I would be quite tempted—"

She leans forward, her last sentence hanging there as if unfinished. I am about to say something commiserating and bland; instead something entirely unexpected pops out of my mouth:

"Of course, we've been hoping you'd be sensible and turn him down." This is what I say! My heart starts racing, and I grip my purse as though it's the safety bar of a roller coaster. "We all sort of look out for Gustav, as you know," I continue, making my hair stand on end. "He has this tendency to overstretch his boundaries—you've noticed—and sometimes the consequences are unfortunate."

I can't go on, and I can't look directly at Vera, although I try to watch her out of the corner of my eye. Is it my imagination, or has she relaxed a little bit? She adjusts the angle of her folded legs and squeezes one foot against the other.

"Do you think so?" she says.

I nod sharply, still not quite looking at her. "Heloise may tell you something different," I add. "But she's always been one to fall for Gustav's grand visions."

She stands and walks toward the ladies' room. I imagine that she looks as though a great burden has just been lifted from her shoulders, and I bite my lip to keep my glee under control. It's a hysterical glee—I feel I could as easily howl with shame as with joy.

· · ·

"So?" Heloise asks me as I sit down again. "What news? Any progress?"

"Well," I say, "Yes. I think so. She was on the telephone." I can smell ham and egg on her breath, and I notice how her whisper flecks me with spittle.

"Oh! What was she talking about? Did you hear?"

"Not really," I say. It's my lingering shock and nervousness, I decide, that has suddenly made Heloise's whisper almost unbearable. I crane my neck to watch the Behrs, wishing I could be up there, straightening Lisa's napkin, making small talk with Martha while Gustav is occupied in charming Vera, smiling and nodding. I imagine Bluff without them, their little house on Oak Street empty and forlorn.

I go to the concert in the evening. This is not unusual; I have season tickets to the Bluff Philharmonic, but my seat—I always sit alone—is in row 42, the mezzanine, from which Gustav, and the rest of the orchestra, is slightly blurry. Tonight I sit in the seats Heloise bought, third row. I can see the worry lines on the faces of the string players, the dandruff on the shoulders of their concert jackets, the ergonomic cushions a few have brought with them onto the stage. It is a little disconcerting to be this close. I try to read the program but Heloise pokes me with her elbow.

"I think Vera's going to do it," she says. "She didn't say anything at dinner but she had that *glow*."

I flush violently, but try to hide it by nodding and peering more closely at the program. The concert format is unusual. There is no major symphony, and the concerto—"Vera's big solo," Heloise keeps calling it—is on the second half of the concert, after the intermission. It's followed by *Finlandia*, the last piece in the concert. Possibly the last piece that Gustav will ever conduct. I am surprised because Gustav has always called *Finlandia* Sibelius's "happy work," clearing his throat slightly before "happy." The Beethoven concerto is the most serious piece on the program tonight, almost as if Gustav meant his final concert to be a tribute to Vera instead to himself and the Philharmonic. For some reason this bothers me, although it might simply be the aftereffects of my talk with Vera. Everything seems unbearable. The stench of the glossy program paper, the scratch of the wool tweed on the seats, Heloise's craning and whispering.

Gustav comes out to applause. I can hear shouts of "bravo" from the audience behind us. It is going to be an emotional concert. Gustav looks as though he is trying hard to keep a serious face, and not grin wildly. He tugs down his cummerbund and coughs. He doesn't look decrepit, I think, suddenly guilty. He looks distinguished.

The first half of the concert goes well. The orchestra seems to be trying harder than usual to concentrate and get things right, although this may be a function of my closer seat. I bite my lip angrily when I remember Heloise's comment about how Gustav feels "shackled" to Bluff. At the same time I know that this is true—I've always known it; but somehow I see it again, closer and stronger, in the way the fabric of Gustav's tuxedo, stretched a little tight across the shoulder blades, jumps every time he signals a crescendo or an entrance cue. I can see the fabric tighten and shift, absolutely in time and almost a music in itself, and I can hear the orchestra follow, muddily. Somehow in the motion of his tuxedo there is both his endless, beautiful patience, and his endless frustration. I remember how I have been scheming to keep him from leaving and I blush again.

At intermission Heloise and I mingle in the lobby. There is the sense of a great secret being kept. A certain excited hush, an impatience, and a glancing back toward the green room. Heloise feeds on it, asking probing questions, making pointed comments, pretending that she too is in the know. For a moment I think I will faint; anything to block out Heloise, who is squeezing my arm and whispering, her voice ugly and hissing.

We return to our seats. Heloise can barely keep still and I feel like I might fall asleep.

Vera strides out, stunning in a red silk pantsuit and a black cummerbund. Gustav follows, smiling. They bow. The clapping dies down and they begin the Beethoven. The flutes are out of tune in the opening, and the violins, when they enter, are thin and toneless. I barely notice them as I stare at her, trying to see if her decision is written anywhere upon her.

Vera stands there, adjusting her chin rest, adjusting the tension in her bow, waiting for her entrance. Her face is focused. She frowns a little, then enters. She looks as though she has forgotten Gustav, like there is nothing now but her and the Beethoven. Her bow strokes are strong, rich, and then suddenly, halfway through a stroke, mild and sweet. She closes her eyes and her left hand marches up the fingerboard, pulsing, vibrating, poking the music into existence.

My emotions switch again. It is for this—to stay connected to this heavenly music—that I have told my lies. And I'm certain that it has worked, that Vera will turn him down.

Finlandia follows, rousing and magnificent. Gustav conducts it almost absently, holding his chin with his free hand, smiling a bit. At the end he bows once and hurries offstage while the audience rises in ovation, expecting his immediate return. There is a long wait, and then Gustav reappears, looking confused and irritable. He doesn't return all the way to the podium to take his second bow but stands at the side, almost behind the cellos. There are shouts of "bravo!" but Gustav doesn't acknowledge them, and he almost doesn't notice the little girl who runs up with an armful of roses. He leaves the stage and the applause fades away. The lights come up and the audience leaves, looking back toward the stage as they go, as if the Maestro might suddenly reappear.

By the time we make our way to the lobby there is an odd buzz about the edges. We see the orchestra manager whispering tensely to one of the board members. The board president rushes past us, down the hall toward the green room. Heloise hangs back, clutching her purse, but I find myself drifting toward the green room. I'm pulled by a curiosity that is stronger than myself. My eyes feel like they're on ice, uncloseable.

Through this haze I can hear Heloise, hovering behind me, saying, "Has she gone and double-crossed us? Is that what this is all about?"

She refuses to enter the room so I leave her in the hall. The room is in shambles. There is a discarded pile of rose bouquets, still in their wrappers, and a Styrofoam cup of coffee has been knocked across the table. Gustav is sitting behind the flowers, talking earnestly; Martha, standing behind him, smooths the front of her dress over and over. At the corner of her mouth a muscle spasms. This isn't the Martha of our teas, or the Gustav, professor emeritus, of the music building. This is something new.

There are other people in the room. In the far corner, the board president and the concertmistress whisper, their voices hushed and serious. Lisa sits on a chair in the corner, her back completely straight. No one seems surprised to see me, or asks what I am doing there; instead, the board president turns to me and says, "Vera's left. Up and ran out after she was finished. I asked if there was anything we could do for her and she said no. Strangest thing. And I think she may have taken Heloise's car."

Martha turns toward me and for once she does not have a cheerful smile or an eye distracted by her children. She looks at me as though she is drowning, and I have a wild image of taking her shoes off and putting her to bed, pulling up the covers around her and Gustav, bringing them a hot water bottle the way my mother used to do for me.

The concertmistress lays a hand on my arm and says, "And the maestro—he hasn't taken it well."

Martha sort of shudders, and collapses into my waiting hug. My nose is pressed into the scratchy purple fabric of her dress, the foam shoulder pad beneath, and the lotiony lavendery smell that is Martha. I am startled by her weight and her warmth. It has been years since I hugged someone.

"Maybe he will listen to you, Meardis," she says, still clinging to my shoulder with one hand. "Maybe you can bring him out of himself. I can't understand it."

Poor dear, I think, of course you will be needing help. Gustav is so much to handle, and then you have Lisa too. The poor little thing. And to myself: *they need me.*

Gustav gestures abruptly, rolling his head back, almost a jovial gesture.

"It's the missing link, the airport," he says. "I keep explaining this."

He looks directly at me, but without focusing. I feel suddenly cold.

"They're not listening, Meary, but I know you will," he says, leaning forward a little. "The airport. We need to call the airport and they won't let her board the plane. It's very simple. Tell them—tell them—that I am Maestro Gustav Behr. They know who I am."

Martha stares at me with helplessness.

"We need to get him home," I say in my library voice, calm and decisive. "Shall I drive, or shall I meet you there?"

Martha is reaching forward, nodding, the soft planes of her face sinking toward me, when Heloise chooses this moment to barge in, electric with nervousness.

"Will someone tell me what's going on?" she says in a resonant voice. "All I want to know is where is Vera, and what has she done with my car? Will someone tell me this?"

There is a lit cigarette in her hand, which is against building regulations, but no one corrects her. She walks up to the board president, ignoring Gustav and Martha.

"I mean, she comes here, screws us all, and takes my car. I mean, right?" Heloise looks at me now, too, smoke coming from her mouth and nose, lips fixed in something that might be supposed to be a smile.

Unconsciously, I think, the rest of us turn to look at Martha, to see what her reaction to Heloise will be. Her face is grim and she doesn't return our gaze. She seems to be summoning something within herself.

"I mean, right, Martha? She's screwed us all? Your husband, my car?" Heloise looks at Martha, and takes a frantic drag on her cigarette.

Gustav swings his head to look directly at Heloise, now, and he sets the fingers of one hand down in a little point, on the table, as if to emphasize what he says next.

"It's not your car that's important, Hel," he says. "She's not driving, she's flying on a plane. And that's why we need to call the airport. So they won't let her board. It's very simple."

Heloise, fixed in his gaze that is so eerily diffuse, takes a step backward. She looks at me. Her hands are shaking. I think they were shaking before but they now are really shaking.

"Jesus," she says to me, in a voice that is not too loud. I nod.

In the stunned silence Lisa's crying becomes audible. She is not sobbing, but her breathing is loud and ragged with tears and mucus. She is looking straight ahead, squeezing the seat of her chair, and her whole face is wet.

There is a hesitation, and I am nearest to her. "Oh, sweetheart," I say, reaching out to take her in. I expect, I think, a hug like Martha's, wetter and sloppier, but tender, with her cinnamon smell. There is nothing rapacious or eager in the way I put one arm around her back, one hand on either shoulder. There is nothing triumphant. But there must be something, because Lisa shrugs me off violently. I feel as though she's hit me.

"I want my mom!" Her voice is angry and thin. She pushes out of her chair and runs to Martha.

Martha inhales sharply and I turn, hoping at least for some recognition of what I've tried to do. Instead, the look on her face is resolute politeness. "Maybe we need to go now, Meardis," she says, then inclines her head toward Heloise. "You'll get her home?" Her hand reaches out for Gustav's and enfolds it. She no longer looks as though she's drowning.

You'll get her home? It's not a question, but an assignment. A relegation. I watch Martha gather up their things—putting on coats and hats, gathering up purses, handkerchiefs, crinkling bouquets of roses. Heloise stubs out her cigarette in an abandoned soda can. Her nervousness has passed and she seems rather remote, as though she is distancing herself from Lisa's outburst at me.

The Behrs go out: a woman in her prime, a fragile old man, and a thin little girl—a family unit, domestic, soft, comforting, excluding. The rainy night air blows in after them. "Well," says Heloise, tonelessly.

"Well," I say.

We do not look at each other, as if our faces are mutually repulsive. There is nothing left for either of us, now, but each other. We pass the catering kitchen dumpsters, and the smell follows us into the car, immense and sour, filling me with unbearable sadness.

Bear

BATTLEMENT MESA, CO. Local guide, waitress, firefighter, and dispatch caller Amy Johnson, 31, died today of injuries apparently sustained while tracking bighorn sheep.

I HADN'T THOUGHT about Millet for years and years until that girl that fell off Battlement Mesa. The day Bob Millet died we had gone up to Red Elephant Mesa to measure winter bear fat, Millet, Todd Aberlie, and I. Wind high, clear, seven inches of fresh snow. Aberlie had five radio-collared bears, two male, three female. We followed the first signal down into a limestone cavern under the aspen. Aberlie was recording and Millet and I took turns going in after the bears. We dug down three feet with the shovel. The wind picked up and clacked the bare branches of the aspen and the first one to go in was me. I pulled tight the strap of the headlamp and I crawled into the hibernaculum and I pulled in there with my hands until I was wedged in beside it and all I could smell was bear stink. When I'd got in far enough I shook my left foot once. Your legs stay out in the forest and when you're ready to come up you shake your right leg. If you need to come up in a hurry you shake both legs. I had my hands on the bear's pelt and if I felt around I could find his ears and that helped orient me. I wiggled my fingers down into the bear's armpit until the fur thinned out and I found skin and that's where I put the temperature gauge. The skin of a bear is soft, not like you'd expect. Soft and smooth and warm even though the bear's pelt is cold.

Next I took the fat sample. I pushed off the bear as much as I could because this is the hard part. You need to go in where the bear's shoulder meets his neck. I had my headlamp on but you can't see very much. I took a big pinch of the bear's skin on his shoulder where the fat gets laid down. You kind of have to blow away the pelt and then with your free hand brush the skin with a topical anesthetic. I was leaning hard on the one elbow and pinching the skin and trying to listen to that bear. This is the part that wakes them up sometimes. If that happens you have to kick both legs and they pull you out fast, or at least you hope they do. I uncapped the needle with my teeth and then I poked it into the bear and drew out the blood and jiggled the needle around until I got to the fat and sucked out some of that. All this time you have to be concentrating on whether you feel chunks of the fat suck up through the needle but also on whether the bear is moving more than he should. Because they always do move, the bears. They are breathing and sighing and sometimes they'll twitch a little like a sleeping dog, and all of this is all right. But you need to be paying attention because there is a way they move that means they have woke up.

My bear didn't move too much. There was once right after I capped the needle and was about to undo the temperature gauge when he kind of stretched his head like he was thinking about waking up. I stopped moving and didn't breathe and in a minute I could feel him settle back down. I pulled out the temperature gauge and I was ready to come out.

Sometimes there's a minute when I'm in a hibernaculum that I wait. I had the temperature gauge in one hand and the needle in the other and I suppose I was thinking if I had left anything in the hibernaculum and going through my mind to make sure I hadn't.

After the bear got Millet it looked like Millet had been waiting too. It was the third bear that day and it was supposed to be my turn but Millet said he tagged this one, he'll take it. He took off his gloves and took the gauge and just before he got down on his belly to crawl in he dropped the gauge and Aberlie said "Don't lose that gauge. I lose that they'll cut this study for sure. Three-hundred-seventy-five clams right there." And Millet whistled and said "More than I make." And he squirmed into the hole and it was a long time. Aberlie said it must be a hard time finding that fat. Then he said hope he didn't jam that gauge when he dropped it, only the way he said it you could tell he was saying hope Millet's not running into any trouble. And then we stood in the cold watching Millet's legs out on the snow. They turned one way and the other as Millet worked. Sometimes he pushed with his toe against the snow and sometimes his heels touched together like he was thinking. Then for a long time they just lay still. And then they gave a great jerk and they weren't Millet's legs anymore but the end of what the bear was biting and we pulled him out and we dragged him fast as we could down the hill and Aberlie was shouting "You okay, Millet? Talk! Talk to us!" and "GO GO GO" to me. The bear put his snout through the hole we'd left and we thought it might come out but it didn't. Millet was dead the whole time of course and the snow was pink in a trail behind us all the way to the truck and when we laid him in the back of the truck we found the temperature gauge in one hand and the needle in the other.

The whole drive back Aberlie just shook his head and said "Goddamn it" and "Goddamn this to hell" and "I don't see why he didn't kick his legs. He was done. When you're done, you kick, right?" And then he'd punch the roof of the truck.

When we got to the hospital we opened up the needle. It had blood in it and fat too though of course we had to throw all that away. After that day Aberlie's study had to be scrapped and he was lucky his job wasn't scrapped too. My job was scrapped but of course I was a temporary so that was to be expected.

"The thing is," Aberlie would say after that, "the thing is he never kicked his legs. I don't see why he didn't at least kick his legs."

I kept the waiting to myself. Before I would have said it's just not something you think of to say and after there didn't seem to be any point. It wasn't something that had any sense to it and I guess Aberlie was looking for sense. Aberlie's big quest is sense.

But the waiting isn't about sense. It's how you wake up in the dark and you lie there and listen to the house breathing and part of you is there warm in the bed with your wife's sleep smells. And part of you is up over the house and watching. And you feel the winter dawn approaching before you can see it and you feel your way down into your boys' dreams and you ask yourself if things are all right with the world and then if things are all right you can go back to sleep. It doesn't make sense but there it is.

So you're there beside the bear. You lie there and you can feel your heart beating against his body cause you're terrified and excited and touching a bear and he's slippery and huge and secret all at once and yes, it's true, you could die. But you listen to the bear breathing and to something else, maybe it's the dark secret interior of the forest. You can take all your measurements but I don't think it ever really tells you what you need to know about the forest. Aberlie would say it did. But Aberlie never went into the hibernacula himself.

Millet knew. And if I had to guess about that Johnson girl, she knew. She knew how you get up so close to them that you're trespassing and when you're there you find that you have to give something of yourself. It's not right to get in so close and slip out. You get there and you have to give yourself to them for a moment and maybe in that moment they take you and that is all right. That is all right.

Otters

THE ANGER AWOKE before she did, a snarly boil right below the surface of her mind. It bubbled out with its familiar index of complaints as Cynthia gathered consciousness—no heat, no gas, no running water, not even a decent bagel within a day's drive—until she remembered her father's letter, and the anger ceased. In the ensuing silence she opened her eyes.

The sun on the trailer wall was bright and flat, like mid-morning—God, it must be almost eight, and Billy was long gone, his side of the bed like a rumpled rebuke. He'd tried to wake her at four thirty, as he did every morning—this was her goddamned project after all, she thought, you'd think she could drag herself out of bed for it, but she couldn't, so he'd gone off to run the telemetry transects himself. He must be halfway through the Lone Dome Road transect by now, driving along at ten miles per hour, with the clipboard taped to the steering wheel and the telemetry antenna sticking out the open window, trolling for the otters' radio-collar signals. Heat blasting, so his fingers would keep working. It was a job just about impossible to do alone, but that was Billy. Always trying to help. Oh, Billy, she thought, as if doing my job better than I can would make me happy.

Cold. The sky was brilliant blue over the mud and scrub and melting snow that surrounded their trailer; beautiful, really, in a completely dysfunctional way. Over her long johns Cynthia pulled a thick hooded sweatshirt, a bathrobe, another pair of socks, and gloves—gloves!— and went down the hall to the main room. This was a mess beyond mess—every inch of surface, outside of the kitchen corner, was covered with tarpaulins. No couch, no coffee table, nothing simply comfortable in all this tangle—only Billy's workbench, his arc welder, and his raft-in-progress.

On a pillowcase beside the workbench were the pieces of the central heating unit, waiting for a part to arrive at Dove Creek Hardware. Normally this sight aroused her anger even more, but today she just thought of Billy's hands, rolling each bolt and coil over with such little boy gentleness. How can such a loveable man be so annoying, she thought, as she shoved her feet into Billy's irrigation boots for her morning pee. She didn't really have the energy to slog all the way out to the privy, so she squatted beside the stairs, propping herself against the corrugated siding of the trailer. I'm some kind of mess, she told herself—in what fit of insanity did I ever think I could survive this winter? And it was only November 3.

While the coffee dripped and sputtered, Cynthia booted up the PC. At least they had electricity—no gas, no heat, no refrigeration, and no running water, but by God, they had electricity. She drew up the folder "Otter Project—North Dolores" and took a sheaf of dog-eared data forms from the inbox, flipping through until she found one that she had filled out. She just wasn't up to dealing with Billy's cryptic scratches, or with that intern's loopy scribbles, which were worse—thank God that ditz went back to Boulder.

Oh, how much she wanted to follow. She missed home so badly it made her teeth ache. Civilization. Away from endless red mud roads, scrub-tree forests, bean farmers, and the huge, deep, echoing canyon of the mighty Dolores, which filled all of her nightmares, waking and asleep. And where seventeen state-bought river otters were swarming free, sending out vague little blips from their radio collars. No, sixteen. Just yesterday they'd found Jenkins's little body—that is, of course, *Lutra canadensis* 93-C-25. The twenty-fifth Canadian otter introduced into the Dolores River watershed in 1993, hit by a car and left to die along Number Ten Road, his collar still sending out regular bleeps. She'd cried when they found him—lord, she was not cut out for this work.

Well, there was always the letter. She checked the computer clock nervously—at least two hours before Billy could possibly be back—and eased open the file cabinet. She'd hidden it deep among the papers on predator-prey cycling models, the mere titles of which could put Billy to sleep. It was three pages typed, well-creased, and gritty with red dirt from reading it out under the pinyons, and it was written on University of Colorado letterhead—her father's peculiar vanity, intensified now that he was angling for vice-provost.

It began commonly enough, with the recap of her father's trip to Venezuela, where he was trying to set up his next dig, and with news of the weather, family gossip, and house repairs. But on page two he got down to business:

> Cynthia, when you wrap up your field work at the end of
> Nov., it's entirely assumed that you'll be coming back to CU
> to complete your thesis, so that you can take advantage of the
> resources, the library, the discussions, the lecture series, the
> whole milieu. I talked with Willis, and he agreed, and he noted
> that there's a post coming open at the university museum,

which would suit you to a T, particularly its being scant on the
field work aspect. I went ahead and spoke with Dr. Scholler,
and she was familiar with your work and seemed pretty eager
to talk to you about the post.

Now, I know your husband has got his sights set on home-
steading in rafting country. That's admirable. But he's got to
understand that a person of your talents and education needs
a more stimulating environment. Plus, I'll be honest, there have
been some concerns about his treatment of you, particularly
the living conditions he expects you to put up with. I'm not
trying to interfere in your marriage. But we want you to know
that no one will blame you if he decides not to follow you back
to Boulder.

There had been a check enclosed as assurance that she would be able
to get back to Boulder, whatever Billy thought. Jesus. Although she'd
cashed the check. The money was in her purse. It had been years since
she'd carried that much cash. She wasn't even sure what she was going
to do with it, only that holding those new flat bills had made the sky
seem brighter, suddenly, as if she could pull out of the bank parking lot
onto the highway, and just keep going. She turned the letter over and
rubbed her forehead. There was that rushing, bubbly, bileish feeling in
her stomach, holding her here at the trailer and pushing her forward at
the same time. Do I have the guts to leave? Do I have the guts to stay?

She took off her gloves, cupped her hot mug, and stared out across
their property. "First real estate I've ever owned," Billy'd said when they
signed the deed. "Most people buy the two-bedroom one-car garage. I
buy fifty acres of mud and pinyon-juniper." Even back then—already a
year and a half ago!—Cynthia secretly would have preferred the cute
Victorian condo west of Ninth, walking distance to coffee shops and
the Sanitas Mountain trailhead, but she was still smitten by the coolness of it. There was a pueblo ruin on the southeast corner, for God's
sake. And elk!

And now look at it. Besides the pueblo, which was just a crescent-shaped hillock, it held three structures—the trailer, the roofless adobe Billy was building for them when winter had interrupted, and the property's original house, a four-room frame and tarpaper affair that was missing a wall. It lay in a private junkyard of broken bottles, tires, oil cans, insulation, and rusted rolls of barbed wire. Whenever Cynthia tried to imagine the people who'd lived here last, she never got beyond a picture of Mayella Ewell's family in *To Kill a Mockingbird*. God, who in Dove Creek wasn't like that? She was becoming quite the snob, she noticed: for every tired, here-come-those-hippies look she got in the Gas & Grocery, she found another bean farmer to despise. And it was the other outsiders and unfortunates she hated the most: those teen moms with six kids each, the man so crippled with Parkinson's he could hardly talk. They were accepted, while after a year and a half people still pretended not to know her. She could see why no one ever packed up and left Dolores County: they fled when they got the chance, taking whatever they could carry.

Which is what she was going to do, here, soon. It was just too much to take. She could feel herself collapsing inside, letting her father's arguments take over. No one ever expects field seasons to be year-round. Mating season, territory establishment: April to September, at most. The winter stuff's known. Entirely without interest, ecologically. Winter's the time to research and tune up your data. I mean, she thought, who cares about the winter months? Billy was the one who insisted on being unique, on toughing it out for a more rounded data set. "Go on," he'd urged, "we can do it. We can make it happen. You'll show all those other students what real researchers are made of."

So of course she felt like a cop-out. But, oh God, she needed a break, before she went crazy, or froze to death, or got stuck in the mud and died of exposure and starvation. "Researcher Found Dead in Rural Dolores County—Insisted on Completing Data Set." "Researcher Dies in Murder Suicide, Melts Husband with His Own Arc-Welder."

Billy was the obstacle blocking her escape, sure as if he'd parked the

Dodge lengthways across the drive. He'd taken root in this godawful mud and flourished: just last week he'd looked up from some project, eyes bright, and said, "Cyn, I really feel like I've found my place here. For the first time."

She'd tried not to scowl, but inside something had fallen down and smashed. Although of course Billy got along, he always got along. There was always some machine thing he could strike up a conversation about—they'd stop in the Dove Creek Hardware to pick up a washer on the way home from running transects, and nine times out of ten he'd be there an hour or more, debating the merits of John Deere over Caterpillar. While she stood by, smiling stiffly, pretending to be involved.

And then she got the letter—fortunately Billy was completely uninterested in anything her father had to say, and never looked into his letters beyond a polite inquiry or two. She'd had to put it aside when she came to the second page because Billy was only twenty feet away, tinkering on his raft, and she thought he might see her heart pounding. "What'd your Dad say?" he'd asked, staring upside down into a piece of tubing.

"Oh, not much, Venezuela trip, permit problems, the usual." She could barely breathe.

It wasn't, she reasoned now, so much that she hadn't thought of leaving Dove Creek before the letter. She had always entertained treasonous dreams, to keep her spirits up when the project was faltering. It was that she hadn't realized before what leaving Dove Creek might entail—*no one will blame you if he decides not to follow you back to Boulder*. In the days after she read this, she kept stumbling against this wall: leaving Dove Creek meant leaving Billy. No matter how many times she thought about it—and she bent her whole mind to it, as if it were a matter of statistics, that would yield to proper analysis—she couldn't imagine it ending any other way.

Say Billy, for example, did follow her back to Boulder. Could she bear to live beside him, every day watching that glow fade a little more, and knowing that it was she who was doing this to him? They could pretend to be happy—rent some beautiful shack up in Sunshine Canyon or somewhere, and play the parts they both used to love so much: Billy the rough-neck adventurer, Cyndi the scholar who stalked mountain lions on weekends. Oh, they could snowshoe and hut-trip and kayak, eat Sunday breakfast at the Lickskillet Bakery, hold parties, cook large gourmet meals, and read natural history around the woodstove on winter evenings, just like they did in the good old days. But Cynthia knew that the life they had tried together, for seven wonderful years and one horrible one, was approaching its end. Just as she knew that her master's project, hard-fought, wrested from the cynical hands of state wildlife officers, was only a dull drop in the provincial tale of Colorado natural history. When the last of the ill-fated otters died, without issue, as was clearly bound to happen, her life's work would be just another failed reintroduction.

Well, I'm certainly not delusional, she told herself sarcastically. But what was Billy going to think? She had to think of a way to get around his usual counter-argument, that personal sacrifice will make anything possible. Her lack of an ability to sacrifice herself would again be brought up as a major flaw, but not an insurmountable one, since he would gallantly step in to take up the slack—"And for what, Billy?" she asked the trailer aloud. "And for what?" So they could spend the next forty years trading places as the unhappy spouse?

It wasn't the broken heater, or the hauled water, or the endless mud that got to her, although these didn't help. It was that looking into the future, that long gray road, she could see nothing but a life of relentless compromise. And when the letter dropped into the midst of that, like a miraculous reprieve, she suddenly saw the chance to live life as it ought to be lived. There was no way, once she had seen that, to turn back. Of course I love you, of course I do. But not this much. And you don't even know what you're putting me through.

But she didn't expect her heart to jump the way it did when the Dodge swung in at the drive. And he was carrying bags, he'd been to the grocery, and the hardware—and the liquor store, God bless him. She almost choked with pity for this cheery little man.

She sat down at the kitchen table and cleared a place to set her hands. Is this what doctors feel when they must go out to the hopeful little family and tell them that their loved one is dead? She could hear Billy thumping around outside—banging on the side of the trailer, what was he doing? He always had to make so much goddamn noise. And then she could hear him splashing and jumping along the muddy, puddly path to the front door. Oh, Billy.

"They got the part!" were the first words out of his mouth.

"They…"

"Dove Creek Hardware! You know, the heater part. I should be able to fix it this afternoon and get the gas turned on again by Friday at the latest. I'll call the gas company right now."

He sat on the folding chair by the door to squeeze off his boots. There was mud on his boots, his Carhartts, his brown denim jacket, and even a little in his hair, dried droplets, as if he'd been standing beside a spinning truck wheel.

"You get stuck?"

"Oh, not too bad, just a little along that road by the river, off Lone Dome Road. You know, the north-facing section. That road's going to be snowed in pretty soon, and you know what that means—snowshoe time! Unless I can round up a snowmobile somewhere—I think Glenn Dunn might have one."

"I was maybe thinking about scaling back this winter. Maybe not going out every day."

"Oh, yeah, then I can definitely talk Glenn into using his snowmobile," Billy answered, shaking out his coat.

"So, anyway," he continued, "I tracked down Elbert and Roberta. They're in their same old haunts, down by Mountain Sheep Point, no big surprises there. I still couldn't find the Brat Pack, so I think we need to try down canyon tomorrow, maybe go out as far as Slick Rock or even Gypsum Gap, I was thinking. It's worth a shot, anyway. But the big surprise is, I did find Molly—waay, waay up Narraguinepp Canyon, can you believe it? Well, I couldn't find her, but I did pick up a signal, and she's the only one that was sort of headed that way. You gotta wonder if she's alive, or if some coyote's dragged the collar up that way. That Narraguinepp's about dry."

"Could be."

He started to unpack the grocery bags, talking louder over their crinkling and the thump-thonk of putting away cans. She didn't get up to help him, but said, "I was sort of re-thinking the whole winter plan this morning. Thinking maybe about working in some more research."

He didn't answer, and he might not have heard at all, because about a minute later he turned around and said, "Oh, hey, some great news. I ran into Doug Diamond at the grocery there. He said the biologist job at Mesa Verde is coming open. Soon, like mid-February or something. He said you'd have a really good shot at it, especially if you go schmooze a bit with the park supervisor before it gets advertised."

She lined up some pens. "Mesa Verde."

"Yeah, yeah. Wouldn't that be great? That place is mostly wilderness area, you know, butt up against the Ute reservation—maybe then we could go check out the spotted owl nest."

"God, for once, can you not arrange things!"

She threw the pen, not at him, but as hard as she could against the wall. Billy stopped with the wine half out of its bag.

"I was trying to help."

His face at that moment looked so incredibly dumb, as blank of thoughts as a cow's, that she wished she had thrown the pen at him. Immediately she thought it back. But it was too late; he had caught her expression of absolute contempt.

"I'm sorry."

"For what?" His voice was stiff, and he turned around and got out the corkscrew.

"What are you doing?"

"I'm not arranging anything."

"Billy . . ."

"You want a glass?"

"No, Billy . . . put it away . . ."

"Now you're the one arranging things."

She rolled her eyes.

"You don't like me, do you? Not really." His voice was high, fiercely casual.

"Billy . . ."

He uncorked the wine—her favorite, a Pinot Noir—and poured a glass, noisily. Why couldn't she just protest that she did like him, she really did, and she loved him, but she couldn't live here anymore? And she did love him, his chapped knuckles, the jaunty way he poured the wine, cupping the base of the bottle.

"I'm thinking I'm going to wrap up the field work at the end of November. I need to start working on my thesis, if I'm going to defend in May."

He nodded.

"You know I love you. You know that, right? Billy, I love you."

He stood against the counter, not moving, not saying anything, not looking at her. She gripped the side of the kitchen table to keep herself from clutching at him, to keep from begging his forgiveness. All she wanted to do was slather him in kisses and tears, to bring back Billy out of that sudden stranger—God, Billy was her only friend here, within miles and miles! Maybe her only friend anywhere.

"So to finish my thesis I'll really need to go back up . . . to Boulder, the resources, the journals, the library . . ."

He looked at her, very slowly but raising one eyebrow a little, as if trying on a joke.

"And I'll be staying here, holding down the fort?"

"You could come . . ."

He looked out into the room, at the arc welder, the raft-in-progress, the heater parts, and the scrub beyond.

"There's so much to move. We'd have to rent a travel trailer—

disinstall the workbench—I still have to find a way to cover up that adobe better. . ."

Cynthia moved up to him very quietly, rested her head against his jacket, and breathed in that wonderful Billy smell—mud, cold denim, cough drops. And for a time, which she wanted to be endless, there was no sound, no movement in the universe except for the fast hammer of his pulse at the base of his throat, right where the bare skin met the collar of his shirt.

The Hitchhiker Rule

WE BLINK AND Hitchhiker Girl's like halfway up the mountain and looking back at us like Whazzup, turtles? Hugh wheezes something prehistoric and I snort because not with *that* sweat is any chick getting anywhere near him, not even me, and Hitchhiker Girl may be wearing my shirt but she's definitely not me, striding way up there with her golden dreads like a goddess of the motherfucking earth, and Hugh says to tell me to break this rule more often, only panting because both of us can barely breathe, and I ask which one, because technically we're on rule number two here. Never leave the road except to party.

Number one being: never pick up hitchhikers. Not since that kid near Leadville puked all over Hugh's new sleeping bag and he tried to blame it on me because I was the one who thought he might have good shit, which he did, but Hugh always forgets that part.

Love this WEATHER, Hitchhiker Girl shouts down at us, or I think that's what she says because the wind is making it hard to hear, and then she maybe says AWESOME IDEA and Hugh kinda shakes back his hair all proudlike cause he was the one who said "Betcha you can't climb that fucking mountain." What he doesn't say is he says this shit all the time and he's totally kidding, only when Hitchhiker Girl high-fived him and said "You're on, dude!" he couldn't back down, and he's been limping and whining the whole time, even as Hitchhiker Girl turns out to be Nature Girl with her "Look! Bear shit!" and "Smell that? Jacob's ladder!" so that it's practically a nature show up here and even Hugh's getting into it, saying "So what's this weed?" and "Who peeped?"

I'm just wondering if this is the start of a new thing when there's a clap of thunder the size of New York City and Hugh hollers like Tarzan. All of a sudden the sky is Absolut Black from end to end and it's the coolest thing I've ever seen, like being in a concert or inside of God and I'm wishing we'd had a hit before we left the Land Rover and then I'm thinking Hugh did have one, and that's why he's all into the nature shit now, when the thunder goes again only this time it knocks us straight to the ground. I say "What the hell, Hugh, did you just push me?" And he says "No, did you push me?" and we drag ourselves up laughing but carefully now and we go over to where Hitchhiker Girl should be getting up too and we're going to ask her what the hell is up with this weather but she isn't getting up.

She's breathing in funny little gasps and her eyes are staring at the rock in front of her face. Hugh's got this look like, this isn't fun anymore and I know she has about thirty seconds before he heads for the Land Rover because if there's one thing Hugh can't stand it's when someone stops being fun.

So I lean in and tell her she needs to get the hell up and it's starting to rain and she smells funny, like sunscreen and hair and something burned, and I touch her shoulder and it makes my hand wet. She looks at the rock like I've fucked it up big time but her mouth says *You've got to help*. And off on the left of me I can see Hugh starting to leave and so I grab her hand to pull her up only all it does is pull her over. That stops her funny panting but also her breathing stops.

Hugh! I yell and he comes but with this look like he's finished with us. He drags Hitchhiker Girl to the trees at least before he says the thing to do here is get help, by which he means the thing to do here is get back to the Land Rover because once we're down to the main road he speeds up and has a hit and doesn't even ask if I want mine. In town we stop a block away from the police station and I'm fumbling at the door when he says to just tell them we met her on the trail.

And I say "Why don't you tell them and I'll tell them she just went down just like that."

Hugh's quiet. Or you can tell them she just went down just like that, I say, and I'll say we just met her on the trail and she must have hitchhiked in or something because there wasn't a car or anything at the parking lot.

"Hugh," I say. "Hugh, we can't just leave her there."

The Land Rover is quiet as three a.m. and the police station just sits there looking at us. Up on those rocks the rain is still raining and Hitchhiker Girl is still there and all of a sudden the world just feels like a hole, just deep, just ugly, just filling with rain and I'm like, "Hugh."

And he's like, "Go on, if you want to."

And I'm like, "Hugh."

And then in a bit he lets go the brake and we ease back onto the traffic and it isn't until we get to Junction that either of us says anything. And it wasn't until later that I remembered she still had my shirt, only by that time it was too late and I wondered what if we'd never picked her up? What if she hadn't had that prizefighter stride and stoplight grin that made Hugh say "Okay, it's time to break my hitchhiker rule." And it's too bad he's gone back to California and isn't picking up my calls anymore because this is what I want to ask him: Why didn't we do something?

Life History of the Four-Foot Moth

Oleanna Aristide

Professor of Behavioral Lepidoptery[1]

Niobeana gargantua—Niobe moth, or, more commonly, the four-foot moth. A large, reclusive moth usually lumped in the order Saturniidae (although see Aristide 1996, 1998). Males resemble females, and both have relatively inconspicuous markings both above and beneath, with

[1]. Previously of the High Plains University Lepidoptery Department until said department was consolidated for putatively "administrative" reasons with the Departments of Colonial Hymenoptery, Interactive Coccinellidae, and, insultingly, Insectivory; the purely political basis of this decision is revealed in the choice to leave the Departments of Arachnidology and Nematology intact. Dr. Aristide is currently attempting to establish an independent Center of Behavioral Lepidoptery, not to be confused with the opportunistic and self-aggrandizing Beck Institute of Lepidopteran Behavior.

a faint paler-gray border and darker gray disks on the forewing; they are to be distinguished from other grayish-brown moths by their great size. Their wingspan has been documented to exceed four feet, and adult females carrying eggs can weigh nearly two pounds. Like most saturniid moths the adults lack mouths and thus cannot eat or otherwise interact with their surroundings. Unlike other moths the Niobes seem to regret their exile and linger around the doors and windows of human dwellings, clutching their mouthless faces as if in grief; hence their name, recalling the grieving mother of Greek myth.

RANGE AND HABITAT: Once thought to inhabit strictly tropical and subtropical regions of North America, *N. gargantua* has been discovered as far north as Cincinnati, possibly as a result of global warming (Beck and Beck 1992), although equally possibly due to the increased import of tropical fruits (Aristide 1993). While most moths are attracted to light, by which they are thought to navigate, *N. gargantua* is attracted to living warmth and softness (Aristide 1983). Whether this is a learned or instinctual behavior is uncertain; it is known that the moths use living human infants and domestic cats to line the nests of their pre-pupate young (Beck 1972), but experiments to determine if heated, stuffed toys will work as well have been inconclusive (Beck and Aristide-Beck 1978). In either case it appears unlikely to harm the infants in any way, and in fact children that have been reared by the moths tend to be gentler and less tormented by ambition than their peers (Aristide 1979). This researcher has long suspected that she was raised by a colony of *N. gargantua* in early infancy, although unfortunately her beloved parents died before she could confirm this. In any case, it is manifest that certain other specialists in the *Niobeana* genus did not benefit from this early mellowing influence (see in particular Beck and Beck 1979, 1982, 1985a, 1985b, 1988, 1992, 1995, 1998, 1999).

The moths were first described by the Spanish conquistadors, although they were quickly classified by the Spanish authorities as a phantasmagoric figment of an inebriated mind, and many an aspiring naturalist had his reputation ruined after claiming to have seen the elusive creature. While it is tempting to dismiss the Spanish authorities as blinded by propriety, it is a curious fact that *N. gargantua* is attracted to inebriated observers, and this researcher has more than once discovered a previously undocumented population by stumbling through potential habitats under the influence of several glasses of expensive wine or liqueur. No protocol exists to describe this calculated use of alcoholic spirits, a glaring gap in the literature.

Several Native American tribes have names for *N. gargantua*, and it is perhaps significant that these names appear to be free of European influence, so that Beck and Beck's (1998) preposterous theory of a European origin for this moth can be roundly dismissed. In particular, I would direct certain doubtful researchers to the pre-Columbian pottery and stonework of the tribes of the lower Mississippi, where a gigantic lepidopteran figure is often seen hovering just beyond the circle of ceremonial dancers, as if waiting for a chance to purloin an infant. There are also the magnificent proto-mounds outside of Big Piney, Missouri, which by the light of the moon so resemble oversized moths of the *Niobeana* genus that they have more than once given this researcher chills, unrelated either to the frost of the early morning hours or the effects of delirium tremens as so cruelly suggested by Beck and Beck (1999).

BIONOMICS AND CONSERVATION: While the adult moths do not eat during the last, protracted phase of their life cycle, they have been known to drink, absorbing liquid through pores in the abdomen, and are attracted to the dregs of red wine, sweet liqueurs, and mango smoothies. Adults have been known to live as long as eight years, spending their days collecting and nurturing the living walls of their grubs' nests and lingering moodily in dark corners, as if wishing to return to that mythic time of warmth and togetherness (Aristide 1995). The moths themselves are solitary and meet only once, cataclysmically, to mate. The females then tend their nests while the males are drawn to open unscreened windows, where they often stroke their antennae along women's earlobes and are severely injured by the sharp metal of earrings and other jewelry, a habit that endangers the future of this magnificent moth.

The simple facts of the Niobe's life history, however elegant, cannot speak fully on its behalf. This researcher instead would point the reader toward those of a poetic turn of mind, who hail this magnificent moth as the patron saint of those destined for extraordinary grief or loneliness; whether this reputation leaves certain smugly "successful" researchers unable to truly appreciate their so-called specialization I will leave it to the reader to determine. Suffice it to say that far from being a mere ecological curiosity of "rare diversity value" (Beck and Wayne 1978),[2] the Niobe moth is a truly unique creature whose loss would leave the earth a bleaker place.

---

2. That Beck and Wayne (a.k.a. "the Bimbo"), now Beck and Beck, had concern for diversity, rarity, or creatures of value may have come as a surprise to their colleagues, particularly as they did not evince much concern at the time for the sanctity of marriage, the upholding of professional ethics, or the personal feelings of anyone with whom they were connected. This researcher hastens to assure the reader that although she once proudly signed her papers "Aristide-Beck," she is now completely indifferent to this unfortunate period of her personal history and can regard the betrayal by her former friends with equanimity (i.e., she is so totally over them).

The Endangered Fish of
the Colorado River

COLORADO PIKEMINNOW. *Ptychocheilus lucius.* Slender, cylindrical, with an endless body and a long, pointed snout. Once so abundant it was the poor man's meat, it was devastated by dams and invasive species. Predicted to go extinct in my son's lifetime but, as it happened, outlived him.

Once the fish grew big as deer and filled the rivers so thickly you could hear them swimming from shore. So say the old timers, at least, the ones who gave it its first name: the squawfish. Even into college, Max would call it that, to needle me—"You and your mamby pamby PC pikeminnow," he would say slyly—but also, I think, he just loved that name the best. The way it squawks off the tongue, two brash syllables to the prim mouthful of what we call it now. I secretly agreed, despite its history, despite the misogyny and racism twisted into it like runoff in a river. The squawfish always felt like *my* fish: the subject of my senior project, my master's thesis, my early years of fieldwork; I was working on the squawfish when I met the engineer. In the long dry years after Max was born the fish was renamed the Colorado pikeminnow, but that name always felt like it belonged to someone else. Perhaps what Max always accused me of was right: I wanted to turn back the clock.

Max as a baby was gummy, devoted, irresistible. The way his starfish fingers reached out to grab my eyes, the way he grunted as he nursed, the way he crawled into bed with us in the middle of the night, all the way into kindergarten. The way he adored Russian fairy tales and colored pencils and baby birds. The way he would line up all of our shoes, pair after pair, curving over the sill and out the door. All of this, and I still felt the pull of the river like an undercurrent of despair. I thought I would never be able to leave him, until I did.

I was an inappropriate mother from the start. Squawfish, I explained when Max was way too young, means, roughly, cuntfish. Trash fish. Fish as easy to reap as the tribal women; like them, though, it held something of itself in reserve. Given half a sandbar and a bit of flood, the pikeminnow made its comeback as stealthy as a woman slipping back into her old haunts. Like me.

This was the story of my life, the one for which I thought Max would eventually forgive me: left my dream job to marry an engineer, had his baby, lived a sensible decade buried in the suburbs and then, against all odds, clawed my way back to work with the pikeminnow, its resurgence mirroring my own.

Bonytail chub. *Gila elegans*. A large cyprinid fish of the Colorado river, growing up to two feet long and reproducing rarely, if at all. Like most desert fish, it is dark above and pale beneath, hidden in both directions. Tail so thin and bony that even nine-year-old Max could grab one in his hand and hoist it from the water.

"How come we never find any little ones?" he asked, and long before

I finished telling him about dams and age classes and functionally extinct he had wandered off, bored of me already. "I'm still talking," I yelled after him. He shrugged as he disappeared into the sage.

His boredom was a weapon, a silent protest against how I made him come to Utah every summer as part of the custodial agreement. "The river is the world as it ought to be," I'd tell him. He would sit shotgun in my pickup and not say a word for 362 miles, as we drove up out of the city, across the mountains, and down into the desert. As soon as we hit camp he would slip away, liquid and alive; he'd chase lizards, pocket arrowheads, and throw rocks endlessly across the water, enjoying it the way I hoped he would. But the instant he caught me watching he'd go sullen.

I spent my off hours straightening his Scooby Doo sleeping bag, rigging the Dutch oven so that we could make pizza on the fire, loading him up with ring pops and firecrackers and s'mores. Still, one mistake and he'd be bitterly against me. "You care about your stupid fish more than me," he'd say, kicking at the fire. "That's why I love Dad more than I love you."

"Did you put him up to this?" I once demanded of my ex, near tears. Through the phone I heard him push his woodworking goggles to the top of his head and sigh before he answered. I could picture the soft sweaty dents beneath his eyes, the sharp smell of cut wood, the way he'd brush the sawdust from his beard before answering, and I had a wave of longing so acute it almost knocked me down.

I could hear him carefully distancing himself from his bitterness. My fault, I knew, but I refused to allow myself regret. The fish had no use for patio projects, soccer games, vegetable gardens or the-game-on-Sunday life, and I had chosen the fish, or what was left of them.

"Max is just a kid," he said at last. "This is about him being nine."

Nine, ten, eleven, twelve: every year I hoped that this would be the one Max learned to love the river, love camping, love me. Instead he perfected the art of the preteen pout. He dropped my gear into the water, my clothes into the fire, my food into the sand. He ran away when I got out the sunscreen and then howled in pain and rage when his back was too raw to sleep. I told myself this was natural; I told myself he would grow out of it. I told myself the nights of sobbing would be worth it in the end.

What Max loved instead was his Gameboy and the bunk bed his dad had built him back in Denver; his TV shows, Domino's pizza and sushi. He loved telling me about all of the things he did with his dad, and all of the things that I did not do, or was doing wrong, or would never understand. "You just don't get me, Mom," he said, in a world-weary imitation of something he'd heard on TV.

"Nor you me," I snapped back.

The bonytail chub, like all cyprinid fish, has a sensory organ other fish don't have. In the end, it was like I sensed the river with an organ that Max and my ex did not possess. I loved the sweat, the stink, the river's algal pull; the slime of the fish, the alkali of the salt flats on either side, the ancient sandstone stained with iron; the ruins, the petroglyphs, the hidden canyons hung with vines. It mystified me that they didn't love it, too.

Now I sit alone in my camp chair after dusk, my daily notes fallen to one side, the tang of DEET keeping the mosquitoes at bay. The air shifts and a breeze pulls along the canyon, bringing the scent of nylon tent and my dinner, a can of maple baked beans cranked open and eaten cold. I once assumed the river was vast enough to be my everything. Now that it is all I have, I find that it is not.

Humpback chub. *Gila cypha*. Evolved to swim the fast waters of the desert river and specialized to breed only in water warm to the touch. Possesses a distinctive swollen hump just above the head. Almost entirely scaleless; back is greenish gray, sides silver, belly white.

The humpback chub has thrived in the recent drought, even as other species have suffered and declined. My colleagues cheer and roar into my winter office with grins as wide as the beers they buy to celebrate. I go along, I chink beer neck to beer neck; I even, when called upon, make speeches about persistence and science and learning to let natural systems do their work.

I believe all that, but the last conversation I ever had with Max lingers in my ears. "A couple of fish, Mom?" he said to me, tapping salsa from his chip, his carpentry calloused pinky curved delicately toward me, as if defining the space he was going to need. "Four fish? That's why you walked out on Dad and me?"

"I never walked out on *you*," I said, my own burrito ashes in my mouth. That was two months before his car failed to negotiate a curve and rammed into a tree, and I never had a chance to explain it further.

I worked for you, I would have said, *so you can have a richer world,* and he would have rolled his eyes. "Things change," he might have said. "You can't stop time, you know."

For so long, I lived upon my certainty. But now I doubt. When I think of the recovery of the humpback chub, all I can remember is how by the end Max and I had almost made it. There were lunches, texts, and phone calls; he talked of making a trip to try the rock climbing spots near my old field camp. But as if on cue I put the fish between us every time. "Aren't you even a little bit glad you got the chance to grow up in God's own paradise?" I once asked him, teasingly.

He considered it carefully, the way he did everything, rubbing the bridge of his nose with the knuckle of his thumb. "Utah made me what I am today," he said at last. "So I give it that. But what I remember was not a paradise."

Razorback sucker. *Xyrauchen texanus.* Distinctive flat bottom and humped back; will grow to a meter long and look like it swallowed a boat. Olivaceous brown above and pale yellow beneath. Smooth.

The razorback was Max's favorite fish. Even on the sulkiest days of his teen hegemony, he would pop up in a moment if we had a razorback in the nets and come over from where he was grumping on the shore about not having service for his phone or not having pizza in camp for dinner. He'd crouch, walking on the slick stones in his sandals as if born to it, his gray eyes intent on the prize, his growing shoulder blades blistering beneath the desert sun.

Once in college he came along on a survey day. "I still think you ecofreaks are just afraid of change," he said, stooping over the net while his breath blew out in frosty clouds. "But if I had to save one thing from 1872, I think I would reach in and rescue this."

The sudden resurgence of the razorback in 2014 shocked everyone and made wildlife headlines all around the world; no matter how far the news traveled, though, it would never find its way to Max. I whispered it to the air instead. *They found some little ones, Max*, I said. *In nine of forty-seven sites. The highest return in years.*

I even made a pilgrimage back to the city, visited the gravestone with its strange clean edges. I stood under the puny hybrid maple tree and leaned in close, but when I opened my mouth, other words came out, raging and lost against the wind. "This is change, Max," I whispered. "*This* is change."

The wind whipped my words away.

Trespassing

THE SMELL OF THE creek catches her as she goes into the house with the crinkly bags from Target. What *is* that? Julia pauses, lifting her nose into the gathering dusk. Water. Damp and algae and mud, even here in the cold heart of November. She strings the bags onto one hand to better crane her neck and smell, but then the dog rushes out, sniffing her feet and wiggling happily, and her son comes to the door worried about his spelling bee homework, and she is hungry, and her daughter hangs at the window and says, "I'm hunnnnngry," and she hurries inside.

Just before bed she opens the front door and leans her head out. She can hear the creek sussing along at the bottom of the yard, but she can't smell it anymore. The suburban street is quiet and it's cold like a wall. She goes inside.

"What was it?" asks Jeff when she gets to bed. He has a pile of papers to grade stacked on the bedspread and he doesn't look up.

"Mental vapors," she says. "How's the class doing?"

"Terrible," he says with a grimace. "I'm beginning to think they would do better if I just left them alone." He goes into a theory of teaching that says that students learn more with minimal teacher time—"it's just a *little* self-serving but you can see the temptation to believe"—and Julia nods, chuckling appropriately, but her mind is lingering with the creek in its dark wet bed.

The next time she sees the creek—which is the next morning, driving the kids to chess practice and listening to an argument about whether it is or isn't fair that SpongeBob Monopoly is for ages nine and up—her gaze lingers on it, as though it has told her a secret.

That afternoon when she picks up the kids, she takes them to the park on the far side of the creek. She pushes them on the swing ("Underduck!" screams Annie happily. "Again!"), spots them on the climbing ropes and the slide, and tosses a tennis ball back and forth with Will, her ear tips burning with cold. He lobs it seriously, concentrating on his mechanics. He also critiques hers: "No, Mom, you raise your arm like this," he says sternly. "You make an L. Keep your elbow up."

She returns the favor of his seriousness and makes a real effort, but her mind keeps drifting toward the water. As soon as she can, she suggests playing in the creek.

It's why they bought this house, after all: she thought they could better bear the affluent sameness of the suburbs if they had a creek at their back. Yet they've hardly done more than glance at it. She'd had fantasies of Will spending his days there, a kind of Tom Sawyer of the Denver suburbs, but the neighborhood kids avoid the water, and he takes his cue from them.

The creek is pretty and small, a rush of tea-colored water narrow enough to leap across. It slaps and sorts a long series of black-coated stones and where the water slows there is mud. The banks are silty and crumbly, with weeds and shrubby things. She recognizes yucca, but little else. We're not in Wisconsin anymore, she thinks, and has a moment of gasping homesickness, of missing their old house at the edge of the forest where the hedges blazed with fall color and the sky reached up an unbearable, unreachable blue. The creek babbles on.

She blinks and the kids are playing, a raucous game that involves slinging big hunks of algae into the weeds. They seem perfect here, uninterested in the geographic shift, as though there is no difference between the constricted suburb and the deep Wisconsin woods. Or like the suburb fits them best.

Her legs get cold and she keeps thinking she hears something upstream, some whisper or footfall. There's a thin dirt trail along the creek; she leans sideways to see how far it goes.

She does hear something. She stands, with the sudden alertness of having heard her name called, except without actual voiced syllables. She checks back at the kids—still throwing algae—and steps forward, onto the path.

It threads its way along a narrowing bench just above the water. She has a vague sense of where it goes: uphill, through neighborhoods and office parks, occasionally plunging through an old ragged pasture that hasn't been developed yet. It is like those fields, a remnant of a rougher past.

"Come."

She freezes. The word is as clear as a language tape and yet it was not spoken. *Come.* She continues up the path, past her neighbors' houses and then beyond, crossing the yards of strangers. She goes until she comes to a little waterfall, where the creek drops over a concrete berm and widens into a small pool. She drops to her knees, her breath warming the crumpled grass, and stares right into the water.

Here I am, she says.

The creek sorts its stones, babbling to itself.

I came, she says. It burbles.

Suddenly, surprising herself, she plunges her hand into the water. It is startlingly cold and she has a moment of electric dislocation as she watches her pale pinkish hand distorted against the dark slime of the creek bed.

For a handful of seconds, a minute, even, the bracing cold water seems to run across her heart and she feels calmer and more soothed than she has in months. Then her hand starts to sting with cold and she pulls herself up, feeling self-conscious. Going back, she is met by Will, his eyes wounded and worried. "Where were you?" he asks, looking past her.

"Not far," she answers, bundling him into the kind of hug she tries to avoid in public, now that he's a big guy of ten. "Get some hot chocolate?"

Over the next few months, Julia chats and laughs with the other moms at the kids' school, and with the neighbors and checkout baggers and librarians, slowly starting to feel known and a part of things. They bought in the most affordable neighborhood around the best school they could find, and Julia always feels a little shabby as she drops the kids off in their battered minivan. But everyone's nice enough, she tells herself.

It's not even the money she minds so much. It's the way the land is an afterthought, a blank slate, an investment opportunity. Since she's neither an investor nor a developer, it's unclear how she fits in.

And then the kids are growing up. Will used to be her little devoted buddy. In Wisconsin, he would trot happily after her through the oak and maple forest, digging up turtles and Dutchmen's breeches; now he pulls the curtains shut and turns on the computer. He has begun to look pinched and wary. He has friends over, but they spend all their time closed into his room giggling over YouTube videos or playing Minecraft.

The creek is still there, whispering to itself as she crosses the bridge. She begins to notice an unsettled, unclosed feeling that seems to have been with her since they moved. Sometimes it's a physical pain, a little unhealed lip of flesh within that catches on things. When the kids are out of the house and she's alone, her mind wanders and she finds herself getting lost on errands, stopping the car to get out and stare at places where horses graze on shrunken hillsides of prairie grass.

She comes to feel she is living a double life. "Did I see you the other day?" one of the moms asks her at pickup. "Climbing one of those trees over by the athletic club—?"

"Oh, I was looking for our cat," Julia lies.

"We have a cat?" her daughter asks with joy; her son squirms, white and sick-looking, and won't meet her eyes as she shepherds him into the back of the minivan. That night at bedtime he asks in a small voice why she was climbing a tree.

"Better view," she says brazenly, and kisses him. She laughs to herself about where she got such a straight-laced offspring, but still. She feels like he ought to understand her restlessness. He can't sit still either, unless he is staring rapturously into the screen of his iPod.

She talks it over with Jeff. "I just feel like he's growing this shell," she says. She doesn't mention how bereft that makes her feel.

"He's the new kid on the block," Jeff says, shrugging. "It sucks, but we've got to keep reminding ourselves that it will get better." Soon his fingers start again, rushing and tapping.

She gets it into her head that if she can just figure out the lay of the land, things will come into focus and she'll be able to feel her way at last. Out on her runs she makes little forays into vacant lots and behind office buildings, trying to trace the patterns of field and brush and creek. Just after the holidays she's climbing down a steep slope under the powerline and slips, getting mud all the way up to her butt. She laughs out loud, but feels like she's made a faux pas at a party. She checks to see if anyone saw her and limps home.

When she opens the door, Will looks up from his work at the kitchen table. His face falls.

"Hey, bud," she says, hugging him sideways. "How's that whale report coming?"

"What were you doing?" he asks, voice barely audible, looking at his papers.

"I took a different way on my run," she says, trying not to feel defensive. "Exploring. Right? Don't you ever do that?"

"It's weird, Mom. Things—"

"Weird? What? The exploring is weird? Or the places?"

"Both," he says in a tiny hot voice, curling into his homework. He refuses to say more.

That night at dinner, when she and Jeff ask how the whale report is going, Will throws himself onto a ball on the floor and screams, "*Stop asking me that!*"

He screams and kicks the floor all through dinner and when they pull him into his room by his pant leg—the kind of thing that used to make him laugh, back in the farmhouse at the edge of the Wisconsin woods—he screams and kicks the floor in there. By bedtime his face is disfigured by crying and his voice is hoarse, but he still won't let anyone come near him, not even to sit up companionably back-to-back, which has always been the best way to calm him down.

"Good *lord*," Julia says to Jeff as she combs out her hair for bed. "Maybe he needs an exorcist."

Jeff snorts with exhausted appreciation, but tomorrow's Wednesday and meltdown or no meltdown, he's got class, so the laptop is perched on his knees. "Or a psychiatrist," he says, and his voice is serious, or it seems so to Julia, and she takes umbrage.

"It's not that bad. It's a tantrum, for Pete's sake. He'll get over it."

"It's been two and a half hours," he says, and just like that, they're in a fight.

She tells him to go do something about it if it bothers him that much and gets dramatically into her flannel nightgown and under the covers. "He won't talk to me," she says, which is close enough to true.

Forty minutes later Julia is almost asleep when Jeff comes back into the room.

He waits until he is settled into bed—a certain self-righteous sternness to his adjustment—with his laptop on his knees before saying, in a low and serious voice, "I think you'll need to lay off the trespassing."

"*What?*" says Julia, bolt upright. "I never trespass."

"You know what I mean," Jeff says, his face lit by the laptop. "We're not in Wisconsin anymore."

She glares at him.

"He says he's seen you. You know, from the bus. And kids say stuff."

"*Say* things? What, does he want a mom who drives around in a white Suburban and a two-hundred-dollar haircut? Would that be conformist enough for him?"

"I'm just giving my observation," says Jeff coldly. "Because that's all he talked about."

Later she tells herself that Jeff is right. The poor kid has a new school, new house, new state, new social world to negotiate, and here she is, the weird mom like a weight around his neck. She vows to stop.

The creek still glitters, black and inscrutable, between the frosty banks of its bed as they drive to school each morning, but she ignores it.

Winter stretches on and despite the laughing camaraderie of the PTCO committees at school and the playdates with a bit of wine and the book club she joined just to do something non-kid-related, she can't shake the feeling that there is something else. Which is ridiculous, but there it is. Things keep breaking in the house and she develops a pain in her ankle—a bone spur? Tendonitis? A strained ligament? She drives along the streets and roads, raw with old snow and mud, and feels desolate and isolated and unsettled. *Get over it, Julia*, she tells herself. *Pull yourself together.* But the long burning ache never goes away.

And the creek. That holds the secret. She becomes more and more certain, even as snow and cold and kid stuff keep her inside. She starts needing the creek like a physical hunger.

When the kids go off on the bus one morning she blows off the PTCO meeting and walks the neighborhood, looking out over vacant lots and power line rights of way. She goes down along the creek and follows the trail defiantly, past the patios and luxury deck sets, until she comes to a fence. The creek slides away beyond.

Two days later she drops Annie at a friend's house and says to Will, "Come with me."

He groans, but he trots after her willingly, almost like he'd hoped she would ask. She leads him down to the creek at the park and then up the trail. He is a little pale, but he follows, picking his way along like he's trying to keep his shoes clean. "Are we supposed to do this?" he asks, and she assures him that it's a public trail. "I never knew it went this way," he says, as they head up the creek on the little footpath. "Are we allowed here?"

It gets stickier when they get to the old pasture at the edge of the neighborhood and they have to cross a fence. She steps right over without hesitation and he does too, obediently, but asks as he does if this is okay. He glances back at the houses. "There's no trail," he says accusingly.

She shrugs and grins. The creek is talking through its bed, a deep long sinuous sound that is like a party heard down the hallway in an abandoned house. They can't stop now.

As soon as they descend into the creek and can't see the houses anymore, Will relaxes. They pick their way up the open creek beneath the sky and from somewhere north Julia can hear traffic. Here at the bottom it is just the water, their breathing, and the sounds they make as they launch themselves from rock to rock.

"Mom," he shouts suddenly. "What's that?"

She whips her head around, wondering if he can hear it, too, the way the creek seems to be calling her name. Instead he points at a little head with a triangular wake, paddling its way along the roots of the willows. "A muskrat," she says.

He stops and watches it and she pauses too, rocking. She is so happy to be standing here in the winter sun with Will, but she can feel the creek continuing on like an unfinished thought, and it makes her antsy.

"Let's see what's up on up ahead," she says to Will, and since the muskrat has gone under the bank, he follows without protest.

"I didn't know there were muskrats living here," he says in wonder. "I wonder what else is here. Are there beavers, Mom?"

"Beavers!" She has no idea. "I suppose there could be. Here, though? I don't know."

They go companionably through the field, the creek so far below the level of the ragged weeds that their heads are invisible. Only to them it feels like the opposite: the outside world of suburbs and traffic is invisible, and all that exists is the creek and the field and the far hazy tip of some tall building.

"See, is this so bad?" Julia asks. She pokes him teasingly.

He shrugs, unwilling to concede but a smile slides through. "I thought it would be something else," he says finally.

Then they get to the end of the pasture. The creek is louder here, insistent, falling messily from a culvert above their heads. Julia starts to haul herself up the muddy bank and Will hangs back. "Isn't it time to go home?" he says.

"Not yet." She grunts as she kicks herself onto the top. They're just getting to the part of the creek she's never been able to figure out and she can feel the unknown territory in her mind like a gravitational pull. We can't stop now, she wants to tell him, but seeing him heading toward a sulk she doesn't bother.

They're in among offices now, in plain view of the plate glass windows. It's Sunday, so the parking lots are empty, but Julia still feels self-conscious as they bypass the sidewalks and angle across the landscape like they own the place. The whispering has returned, a deep urgent ache just beneath the surface of the day.

She can feel Will withdrawing and she chucks him on the shoulder. "When we get home we'll have hot chocolate," she says in apology. He glares.

"We're figuring it out," she explains to him. "The lay of the land. This is the creek that runs past our house: doesn't it make sense to know where it's coming from?"

He frowns but seems to accept this, smoothing out a little.

The creek drops under a decorative footbridge, skirts a firehouse, and then slams straight into a double culvert carrying it beneath Quebec Street. The passing traffic makes the culvert vibrate. Julia hesitates a moment and then ducks into the drier of the two tubes.

"What?" gasps Will in disbelief. He goes in under duress, clutching his elbows.

On the far side of Quebec, the creek's character begins to change. They pass through the scrim of offices and enter another old field, a darker one, more serious, with scattered trash like mattresses and broken armchairs blown in from the interstate. The creek broadens, spreading out through cattails and muck. Will steps in a boggy spot and sinks his foot to the ankle, coating his shoe with gray mud. He shrieks and rears back as if struck by a snake; she hurries back to make sure he's okay and sighs when she sees the mess. She sighs again when she realizes what this means. She throws one glance in the direction of the creek—we must be almost there, she thinks, swallowing her impulse to just keep going—and then yanks Will's shoe off to dump the water and wring out his sock. The water is icy. They'll have to go back. She says this even as part of her thinks blackly that if he was just a little older he could do it, wear the wet sock and warm himself by walking.

"Here," she says, trying to get the shoe on. She's being rough and Will has gone silent, staring at the creek as though there is something under the water. "Hey bud," she adds, and he shakes himself, coming back. He pushes his cold foot into the shoe and they turn toward home. She only looks back once.

"Where'd you guys go?" Jeff asks later, after everyone is warm and fed and the dishwasher shucks and hums in its little nook under the counter.

"Up the creek a bit," Julia answers, leaning her head back into the couch. She doesn't want to talk about it; just thinking the word creek makes her restless, unsettled, unfinished.

"Will seems better," he says. Will was quiet at dinner and stayed away from his electronics—not so much to engage as to stare into space. Lobotomized, she thinks privately. But she nods.

"We were feeling so unconnected," she says. "We needed that." The words feel like a lie in her mouth and she gets up to remind Will to brush his teeth.

His room is warm and clean and he's standing at the window with his back to her. It's so familiar, this room, and yet strange: it's his, where he's trying to set out the boundaries of himself, and there's part of it that isn't accessible to her even if she reaches out and moves it with her hand. There's his beloved iPod, kept on its own shelf just above his bed. His books, each series kept carefully in order. His matchbox cars, sorted by color into boxes. It is all so careful and so organized and yet she feels it is missing something of *him*, of Will, of the eager, goofy boy who used to tag along with her on hikes. Is he better? She can't tell.

"Bud?" she asks, and he jumps and closes the curtain over the night.

"Why did we pick this house?" he asks, scowling. "Everyone says this is a dump street."

"But it has the creek," she says. Her cheeks sting. Those spoiled little brats at his school—

"I hate the creek," he says, but his face struggles with it. "There's something wrong with it."

"Stop walling yourself off," she snaps, surprising herself. "You're becoming a real suburban brat and it makes me sick."

Over the next few weeks she keeps catching herself being spiteful. Whenever she finds him playing video games she sighs with irritation and makes him turn them off. He invites a new friend over and she tosses them outside. "Play out there," she tells them, and practically pushes them out. Then she watches them wandering desolately within the confines of the yard, throwing wistful glances at the door and making half-hearted stabs at playing with Will's foam dart guns. When she finally relents and calls to them to come inside they drop the guns in the snow where they stand and bolt for the door. Jesus, she mutters. Will doesn't look back but she can tell he hears, a certain way he both deflates and amps up, calling too loudly to his friend that the zombies on this game are the *sickest* ever, they are the *boss*, aren't they so sick?

I need to let him be who he is, she tells herself sensibly, and then is blindsided by the fury that descends on her: why can't *they* let *me* be who *I* am? None of them do, not Jeff, not Annie, certainly not Will—she shuts the thought down quickly, but the bitterness permeates everything.

School is crazy again, working up toward spring break, and the kids are both in sports; between practices and games they don't have a minute extra. It's suddenly obvious why the kids around here never go outdoors: in order to be outdoors, you have to have idleness, and no one here is idle. She feels chastened, like she's finally noticed something obvious. They aren't in Wisconsin anymore.

In between, like background noise, she still hears the murmuring of the creek. It makes her intensely irritable and she wishes she could turn it off. At the same time, whenever she sees Will turn away from it deliberately, for a split second she flares with anger.

One afternoon when she's made him play with Annie she overhears him teasing: "The creek is annngry, Annie," he says, his voice sly and mean. Oh, Buster, you are so busted, Julia thinks, but is stopped short by the next thing he says. "It talks to me," Will whispers. "It says, 'I'm going to *get* you.' It says, 'I'm going to *get* that little girl, too, your *sis*ter. I'm waaaatching you.' You can go ahead and tell Mom, Annie. But she won't care. She *likes* the creek." Annie comes to her in tears, but won't repeat what Will said. Julia wonders what other secrets they have been keeping from her.

After dinner Julia goes down to the edge of the yard. It feels strange to be listening to the water after so many weeks of pretending it doesn't exist and she watches herself with a distant and clinical eye: just another woman picking her way down the garden path in the dark. Only this one has a certain eager catch in her step, an illicit hastiness.

Then, at the fence, she is hit by a wave of longing so intense she can't tell whether it comes from inside her or beyond her. The creek seems to be rising up above its own bed, something in its babble grasping and raw. Its loneliness reaches up out of the muddy banks, a rusty clutch of misery, and it is like she has unexpectedly caught sight of her own reflection. She backs away.

That weekend the fields are too wet for games. When the clouds lift mid-morning, she heads out and starts hacking brush from the hillside. It's all weeds, cocklebur and knapweed and prickers and thistle, and the creek in its little bed seems innocent again. She makes Will help her instead of playing on his damn iPod. She threatens to take it away. "How can you just pretend we don't even have a creek?" she asks, ripping at weeds, her voice pitched a little too high and a little too loud. "I would've killed for a chance to live next to a creek like this. I would've loved it. I would've been out here every day. It's like you don't even know how to play." She feels him watching her, baffled and abject. "Mom, that's not true," he says miserably, and his voice cuts her to the quick. Still she cannot let it go.

"How isn't it?" she asks bitterly, and behind her he is silent. After he leaves she stares at the ground in self-loathing, then goes inside without putting anything away.

That night a late spring storm moves in, howling up the creek, making the trees overhead shriek and clack. It comes with snow—two inches, then five, then more rain that washes it all away. The creek, swollen with melting snow, roars in its bed, huge torrents that seem to slam against the bank, almost straining the foundations of the house. Julia pauses as she chops carrots for dinner, wondering if she should be worried. But she leaves a window open; even though the sound unsettles her it makes her feel alive, to have this beast roiling and cracking just outside.

Meanwhile, the kids are worked up. They are fighting over everything; she asks Annie to set the table and Will to pour the milk and they argue over who gets to stand in front of the silverware drawer. "Don't use *those* forks," Will says archly and Annie hisses at him. Then there is a scuffle in the dining room; Annie screams that Will is throwing everything to the floor. "You're doing it the wrong way," he yells.

Julia tells him to cut it out and he throws the forks on the floor again. "You hate me, just like it says," he sobs. "You love Annie but not me. Maybe I *will* just go—"

The creek roils and strokes just beyond the window.

"Go what?" asks Julia, but just then Jeff comes in, looking irritated, and says no one should say one thing more until they eat. Will makes a ludicrous face at Annie and mouths, "This is all *your* fault," and Julia tells him to go to his room, right now, I don't care, immediately, or I will take away your iPod for a fucking month. He shrieks like an animal.

"You, too," Jeff says to her. "Not another word."

She bites her lips closed and turns back to the half-made salad. She is shaking with fury. The creek is louder than ever; it tears at the hillside like it wants something, like it is demanding to come in. Julia slams the window shut.

"Just get the dinner on the table," Jeff says, and grimly comes to help her get the lettuce into the bowl, the carrots sprinkled, the pasta dished out. The silence between them is so intense and heavy that they do not notice the absence of Will until it is too late.

Jeff springs to the front door so quickly that he knocks over a chair. As *if*, thinks Julia, but there is a pit of dread at the bottom of her stomach.

"Where is he? Will?" Jeff whirls around wildly and that's when they see Annie standing behind the door, shrunken and terrified. "Where did he—"

"He didn't even let me," Annie says in a tiny voice. "He said I was too little. He wouldn't let me."

"Oh, sweetheart," says Julia. "He didn't mean—" But she breaks off. She has no idea what Will meant, or what Will is doing, and she senses they have set forth into something new and terrible.

She takes a coat but Jeff refuses one, brushing her aside to plunge into the storm. She follows numbly, her head buzzing.

The roar of the storm is enormous and her head turns toward the immensity that is the creek even as she follows Jeff down the front sidewalk. He is a black shape against the gray sky and then he is a stooping shape, a turning shape; he tosses something to her. She thinks it is a softening until she catches what he has flung into her hands: Will's glove, soaked and muddy.

"Don't just follow me," he says, and it feels like the last thing he will ever say to her. She watches him flail into the dark, shouting Will's name.

The glove's sodden fabric is even wetter than the sleet pouring from the sky. She puts it in her pocket like her own self-loathing and heads down the hill, toward the creek.

She picks her way between the houses toward the swollen water. Light glints back in weird places, the water sickeningly high and fast. Would he even go this way? she starts to ask, turning back to go after Jeff, but the rain hits her face like a wall. Just look anyway, she tells herself in Jeff's voice. Bother yourself to fix what you goddamn broke.

She goes on, choking with fear. How can he be out in this? Was he even wearing shoes? Her panic plugs her directly into the night and these feel like equivocator questions, like deep in the stupid sweaty part of her brain she is trying to negotiate the dimensions of her failure. Bottom line: her boy is out in this. She drove him there. Does she even deserve to live?

Deep in the trees where the creek pours, something slips away, white and wet. "Will!" she calls, bounding forward. But the thing has vanished. Twigs and prickers catch at the fabric of her clothes and the knees of her pants are so wet that they pull at every step she takes. The ground is treacherous where the creek is eating it away and the creek itself roars through its bed like an interstate highway. Or like oblivion.

The night is striped with long bands of light from her neighbors' houses, where inside the families are warm and whole, feeding themselves on the fat of the land. Over the storm it seems she can hear them chewing, swallowing, whispering to each other, their immense self-satisfaction like grease running down their backs. Meanwhile, she is a monster, a wretched thing howling in the weeds.

The street emerges from the rain. She has made it to where the creek crosses under Maple Lane, and she comes unsteadily up into the light of the mercury vapor lamps. A commotion up the block catches her eye: someone comes flopping across the street and connects with a small and reluctant shadow hovering in the lee of a parked car. *Jeff.*

And the shadow is Will: she watches Jeff strip off his sweater and wrap it around Will, and the joy runs through her like water. She calls out to them, waving, but between the rain and the dark they do not notice. They turn and leave her, walking back toward the house. I should go to them, she thinks, but does not move.

Instead, when they have passed out of sight, she crosses the street and peers up the hungry roar of the creek where it pours out of the vacant field, and beyond that offices, and beyond that the enormous broken prairie beside the interstate, where the creek begins. In the dim light of the streetlamp she can see that the sleet has begun to collect on the grass beyond, pale and translucent. No Trespassing, says a new sign, and she reads it with relief: no one will hold her back this time. She slings one leg over the rail and then the other.

Appletree Acres

MY MOTHER BLAMED the selling of the Beckett farm for Missy's murder, and while I couldn't quite connect all the dots when I repeated this argument to the kids at school, I knew it was true. When the school bus rounded the corner of Beckett Hill and there was the earth scraped bare from here to the highway, all I could think was what my mother called it: an abomination. Some days you could smell the strange new mud from the little wood behind our barn, which was my favorite place in the world the year I turned twelve. Abominable, I would whisper, lying on my back among the mayapples, and if I was feeling particularly self-pitying about it, a few tears would roll down the sides of my eyes. *Abominable.*

This was before anything happened to Missy, so the abominations were all against me, or my family. There must have been a few other people in the valley who were appalled when the Beckett family decided to get out of the farm business, but they kept their objections to themselves. My parents, self-proclaimed loudmouth professors from the city, claimed to be the only dissenting voices at the community meetings about Appletree Acres. No one listened to them anyway. "They'll be so sorry," my mother said, shaking her head, when they came home. Appletree Acres was going to be a planned community on the newest model, housing three thousand families, a clinic, three schools and six shopping districts, all in planned array with bike paths, a nature preserve and a golf course. "These people, they think it's all about shopping and property prices. What they don't understand is how it's going to ruin everything. Traffic, crime, urban transition pathologies..." She sat down on the edge of a chair, still in her coat, and shook her head. Dad briskly shook the snow from his coat. "Not to mention the environmental mess," he said. "They're dreaming if they think that nature preserve is going to mean anything when it's surrounded by houses."

"The herons..." wailed my mother softly. Dad nodded, mouth grim.

Six months later I could hardly find a spot on our land that wasn't infiltrated by the grind of engines or drifting exhaust. The wood thrush and song sparrows still sang their lazy, late summer songs, but they seemed jumpier than usual and kept whipping around. Then in October my parents found a man bathing himself in our pond and I wasn't allowed to wander the woods alone anymore.

It was getting cold by that point, so I didn't mind, plus seventh grade had so much homework that I was rarely free before dark. Then there was my new fascination with Missy-from-the-bus-stop.

I had known Missy for forever. As long as I could remember she and her brothers lived across the road in the shoddy chaotic duplexes carved out of the Beckett farm a generation earlier. My parents were rather patrician about them: "...such vigor," my mother would murmur when we drove by and one of Missy's older brothers was careening off an improvised ramp into the road. "Such scrappiness." And then the boy would yodel something profane at us, half grinning with a red Kool-Aid stain above his lip, and we would both shudder. At the bus stop the boys were more of a trial and for a time I insisted on being driven to school.

I'd always lumped Missy in with the boys. She was two years older than me and always gravitated up, so that she was the one laughing hyuk hyuk hyuk at their stupid needling comments or trying to follow along on her too-small bright-pink bike. Her family tended to distinguish itself for its brawling skills rather than its academic ones, but she in particular, perhaps because of her relative closeness in age to me, I always found easy to dismiss as a class A dummy.

But that fall I'd started to notice her. She was still all pointed chin and awkward, sidling laugh, but she didn't have brothers on the bus anymore and had to stand alone. One of the things that changed was that she started to talk to me. Sometimes she even sat beside me on the bus—I had my biology textbook open for some last-minute studying, but she'd lean over it as if it wasn't there. "That's where Darren Higgs drove his sister and him into that lake and drowned," she'd say, casually, as we passed our pond at the corner of Stillwell-Beckett Road. Or: "That used to be a house but it burned down, mom and baby inside," as we passed a telltale lone chimney.

Sometimes she would talk about herself. "Got a hickey last night," she'd say proudly, pulling down the collar of her shirt to show me the welts. Or: "Danny's friend says he's gonna let me drive his car." Her conversation was always like this, bragging and smug, infuriating, unbelievable and impossible not to listen to. "My da says if you do it under a full moon your baby'll be a werewolf," was a typical pronouncement. I was still a little vague on the nuances of "doing it," but the biologist in me rebelled at the werewolf part, which she pronounced werewuff. "That's totally ridiculous," I'd say, and she would insist that no, it was true, she herself knew someone who'd had a werewuff baby. We'd argue about it all the way into town.

But the thing that cemented her in my fascination was when she started to talk about my house. First it was our land: "You still have that rope swing out by the old crick?" she asked. "The one in the half-dead tree?" She had a way of watching me, sly and assessing. When she saw how much it bothered me—the swing was in the middle of my favorite wood—she smiled and added, "I made that."

"*What?*"

"I did. You know how the rope has like a little blue thread in it? I found that. It was in my uncle's barn. My brothers strung it up."

The next day she was complaining about her morning shower, which had run cold, and which was so loud that it woke everyone up and pretty soon they were all tramping into the bathroom and peeing all over the seat.

"They come in while you're in there?" My family members were strictly guarded in their privacy and this shocked me.

But Missy half shrugged, half winced, and looked out over the fields. "Small house," was all she said. Then: "Not like that bathroom of yours. I useta love that room, all white, with its big window and the tub with the bird feet. I useta think that was the best bathroom in the world."

This demanded an explanation but Missy ignored my question. "My favorite place though was the closet under the stairs, the one that starts with a door for shorties and then you crawl in under the bottom shelf and there's that little private room back there that nobody can get to and nobody can find you, ever."

I looked into this as soon as I got home. Sure enough, in the closet upstairs, behind the shelves, there was a space. If I moved all of the towels I could just wriggle in and curl up there, awkward but contained. My head had to rest on the back of the stair so the nails poked into my scalp, but this discomfort was nothing to the thought that Missy knew the inside of my house better than I did. I wondered if her brothers knew, too. I decided not, but this conviction wavered in the middle of the night when I couldn't sleep and stared at the plaster fleur-de-lis along the ceiling. These had always felt maternal and protective, but now seemed like hired men, their loyalty lasting only as long as we paid up.

I pulled the covers up over my head and whispered that I hated Missy Mettinger, like, so much.

On Monday she showed up at the bus stop with a keen-eyed grin and another thing to brag about: "Look, Paul Raeburn totally gave me a friendship bracelet! You know what that means!" She shimmied and half lost her balance.

"When did you come inside my house?" I asked in response. She rocked back on her heels with a little smile, kind of like why'd it take you so long.

"I used to live there," she said. "Back when Gramma was getting ready to croak. And we always used to visit before. Since she was born in that house and all. Dad always thought he was gonna get it. Boy was he pissed when he didn't. Drank for two weeks straight, crying the whole time. Still does, when he's had a few." She giggled merrily at the thought, or at my face, which had suddenly stopped working.

"What, you thought you were the first to live in that house? Since when was you a hundred years old? My great great grampa built that place."

Of course I knew, in theory, that I had not lived in the house my whole life. We drove past our old bungalow every time we went into the city to the symphony or the museum. But the thought of Missy Mettinger—and worse, her passel of Kool-Aid-stained brothers—living in my house upended how I had always thought of the world. Missy Mettinger came from a *farm* family?

For in my head I had developed a certain hierarchy. At the top were the pioneers who'd been here from the beginning. Their names were in the rural roadside cemeteries and on plaques in front of cabins. Just below them were the longtime farm families who had their names on roads and towns, like the Becketts. These were the ones who *knew* this place, who felt it in their bones: where the morels sprouted after rain and the nut-dropping shagbark hickories grew, where the bobcats denned and which houses had been stops on the Underground Railroad. Then there were the people like me and my parents, people who were not privileged to have been born here, but who brought a certain sensibility, a well-developed appreciation for the value of the place.

Then there was the rabble, the people neither attached nor appreciative, who'd moved in because it was cheap or because they had run out of gas. Trash, I thought, snobbishly. Hillbillies. Like Missy and her brothers.

I could tell that Missy was pleased as anything at my discomfort, but she had the cunning not to say a word. When we got on the bus she changed the subject. "Sure got a lot of guys out on Appletree these days," she said as we passed the construction site. "Some of em are pretty fine, too. Lookit that one."

I had no desire to "lookit" any of the workers or anything else on the stripped hillside.

"I wonder where they all come from, anyway?" she asked, musingly.

"Urban transition pathologies," I muttered darkly.

She lunged over my lap and yanked down the bus window. "Oo-ee, sailor, you so fine!" she hollered out, pressing her bosoms against the glass and waving a white hand out in the frigid air. The men, what I could see of them from where I cringed in my seat, waved back with bemused expressions. The bus driver told her to sit down. "There will be no whores on this bus, young lady!"

"Who you calling whore," Missy said in response, but under her breath. "You the whore. Old hag."

The new population did, in fact, add a level of inconvenience to everyday routine. The man washing up in our pond was just the beginning. Now we had to wait at the town stoplight when a shift was getting off, and there were long rowdy lines at the gas station. Strange trucks would shortcut through our private tractor lanes and once, walking through my wood in sight of the house, I found a few cigarette butts and a soda can, which so horrified me I could barely pick them up. Finally my parents posted bright No Trespassing signs every one hundred feet. "I hate this," my mother said, tearily. "I feel like the Man."

"It's just for a few months," my dad assured her. He did not sound sure.

Missy, on the other hand, seemed to have waked up.

"I saw that cute one at the feed store," she would say, nodding as we went by. "He knew who I was, too, I could totally tell. He was checking me out, like looking me up and down, like this." She mimed it.

The workers were straggling into the worksite from their trucks. They watched the bus go past and I shrank down, staring at my hands. This used to be one of my favorite views, the fields tilting to the creek, embraced by forest, with the rocky limestone bluff rising beyond. Now it was ruined.

Missy was still talking, in that voice where she bragged by pretending to complain. "—so my da was all like, Sure! You can sleep here! And I was like, seriously? I have to make dinner for two more guys now?"

"Your dad is letting the workmen into your house?"

She smirked. "He hooked up with some guys that was driving in from Dayton. 'It's so faaar,' he said. Really he just wants some more cowboys to ride dirt bikes with. He sure likes having buddies around." She got that vague aching look she sometimes got. "I tole Paul he better be jealous."

"So did your dad really used to farm?" I said, not wanting more stories about Paul.

She brightened. "Oh, sure! Born and bred. Used to drive his tractor to school." She mimed driving a tractor, flinging out her elbows and making loud farting sounds with her lips.

"But you guys don't even garden or anything."

She snorted. "Gardens! That's the last thing a farm is. *Garden*. That's a good one. Nope, we lost it to a buncha richie riches. Cut it in half and sold it. The other half went to the Becketts, which look where it got them."

It took me a while to realize that *we* were the richie riches. It didn't make sense—we weren't rich. We weren't even well off. I was about to explain this to Missy when we pulled into the school parking lot and she bolted out of her seat. "Later, alligator," she said as she went.

Just before Christmas break, Mom was driving me home from choir practice. Construction had ramped up since Thanksgiving and now there were huge lights out on the site and more trucks than ever on the roads. At the latest community meeting some residents had begun to agree publicly with my parents. An elderly local woman was killed in a head-on collision with a drunk man in a pickup, and it had come out that the man was employed by Appletree.

"They should at least have widened the roads," Mom exclaimed as we pulled practically into the ditch to avoid a dump trunk. "I mean, how hard would it have been to predict this?"

"Mom, are we rich?" I asked.

She laughed out loud. "What do you think?" she asked.

"Missy said we're richie rich."

Mom quieted right down. "It's all a matter of perspective," she said. Then, after a brooding pause: "Do you associate much with Missy?"

Her eyes searched out mine in the rearview mirror. "Not really," I said. I didn't add that as soon as we got off the bus Missy pretended not to know me.

"That Missy . . . she's a ball of fire," Mom added, almost to herself. I wondered if she knew that Missy used to live in our house, and if this was news I even wanted her to know. I suspected, too, that we were richie rich on some level.

After Christmas the break stretched long and lazy and I hardly thought of Missy or school or even the construction. A blizzard shut work down for a week and deep in the warm house with the darkness glittering outside things seemed as they had always been. I watched the fields gleam beneath the half moon and imagined we were pioneers, alone in the valley with the snow. It would have been cold but beautiful, I thought. And pure.

The first day back to school the bus stop was empty. Just me, no Missy. I surprised myself by being disappointed; I wanted to ask her what the workmen in her house did at Christmas and be appalled at her answer. Instead I had to get out my biology book and study.

The next day she was still absent. There was a hush and a tension to the whole school and I saw short plump Mrs. Blevins rushing down the hallway in tears. During lunch I heard Sheri Price cry *Stabbed?* two tables over.

I looked around to see if Missy was in yet; sometimes she came in late. She's gonna be bummed, I remember thinking; something big is going down and she was missing it. Also, I was missing it, thanks to her being my only reliable source of information. I felt a pang of irritation. Why, of all days, did she have to miss *this* one?

When I got off the bus, Mom was waiting with the car. This was highly unusual, even with the temperatures as low as they'd been. She looked distracted, but smiled when she saw me like I was five years old again. I declined to ask her what was going on; she never knew what was happening in town, and even when she did know, she didn't believe in spreading gossip.

Instead of heading straight home, Mom asked if I wanted to go for ice cream. "It's sixteen degrees out," I said suspiciously. "Don't you teach on Thursdays?"

"Class doesn't start until next week," she said. "And hey—I thought it might be nice if I hired someone to be here when you got home?" I didn't say anything. I'd had an after-school babysitter when I was younger and I didn't want another bland, weird-smelling woman staring at me while I did homework.

Even though I hadn't said I wanted ice cream she headed toward town. I looked longingly the other way, toward the house, and had a shock. "Why is there a police car in front of the Mettinger house?" I asked.

My mom mumbled something. "I think one of them hit a dog," she said vaguely.

I decided I'd look Missy up in the phone book when we got home. It was a eureka moment for me: I finally had a plan to get around all of this adult obfuscation.

Even at Bob's Shakes, Dogs, and Cones people were acting weird. Two waitresses hovered in a corner, whispering, and when one came over she exchanged a meaningful look with Mom and said, "Isn't it a shame?"

Mom practically fell out of her chair giving her the ixnay on the ixurderay sign, which was totally stupid, since I was the only one around who knew any Latin, pig or otherwise. The waitress added, "They say it was one of the guys at Appletree. They've got everyone out and they're going through pickups one at a time. The manager is *pissed*."

Mom shook her head. "They ought to be placing the blame at the top," she said. "Whose grand idea was it to bring two hundred single men out to the middle of nowhere and give them all these half shifts and open-ended breaks? This kind of thing was going to happen eventually."

"I never liked how some of them stared at me," the waitress agreed. "Gave me the creeps. But I never thought they'd do *this*." I waited until she was back in the kitchen before asking "Mom, who got murdered?"

She was silent for a minute. "They don't know for sure it was a murder."

"Mom!"

She squinched up her face in some sort of grimace conveying delicacy and regret, and put her hand over mine. "Honey. It was Missy. From across the street. They found her body this morning."

The room got very small and the table very big and when my hot fudge sundae came out a few minutes later I couldn't eat it. I poked around the side, moving the cooling fudge along the melty ice cream. Mom watched me silently, her face frozen into an expression that was perhaps supposed to display pity, or else sympathy. I couldn't look at her.

"I didn't know that," I said. She nodded quickly with a huge up-and-down movement.

"I wish I had known that," I said. And I could see her hair moving as she nodded again. It seemed as impossible to eat the ice cream as it would be to eat the booth. I felt, rather than heard, the waitress come inquire, and Mom stage whisper that I had Just Found Out. The waitress started to sniff a lot and the ice cream was taken away.

We went home. The police car was gone, and Missy's duplex looked both abandoned and blown open, even though nothing about it had changed, except that all the snow in her front yard was trampled down.

"I bet they didn't even hit a dog," I said to Mom accusingly, and she nodded. "Why do you always lie to me?" I asked, and didn't wait to hear an answer. I went upstairs to the closet under the stairs and crawled all the way back behind the towels, where I sat with my knees drawn up while Mom stood in the hallway and called that she was sorry, that she apologized, that these things made her uncomfortable. I looked at the back of the towel shelf. Whoever had painted the shelves hadn't always gotten the paintbrush all the way over the back edge and there was a wavering line of bare wood. Someone had traced the edge of the paint with a pencil and there was a line of heart stickers stuck along the back of the second shelf. Missy, I thought immediately. The air in the closet suddenly became very thick and I had to get out.

Over the next few weeks I pieced together what had happened. Missy had been found on a dirt road near the highway. She was naked and barefoot and had died of exposure. This only made me more confused: How were people calling that murder?

The grownups were impossible. Mom sighed and looked disappointed any time I'd ask. Dad would get down to my level as if he were going to tell me the truth, but would only give me vague curling replies. I couldn't bring myself to ask a teacher. When I was getting my hair cut the lady started talking to another stylist about it—"those tire tracks followed her footprints for four miles. You could see where he'd pin her against up the fence and then let her go. Barbed wire prints in her back"—but when I straightened and said, "Are you talking about Missy Mettinger?" she shut right up and I saw their eyes meet in the mirror. The look on her face was something more than an adult protecting a child, something more than disapproval at my inappropriate curiosity. It was a closing off. Like they were protecting Missy from me. There in the chair I felt myself turning hot. *Buncha richie riches.* That was how everyone thought of us. The entire town.

If this had been a movie or one of the after-school TV shows I had taken to watching before my parents got home, I would have leapt up out of the chair, my hair still wet and half cut, and run out onto the street. The screen would have faded to the glare of sunlight bouncing off cars. Instead I looked down at my lap, where little bits of hair clumped and scattered over the smock, and felt like I was made of wood. I cringed when my mother came in to pick me up, greeting the ladies by name as if she knew them. *You will never know them*, I thought. *They will never let you.*

The death of Missy came down in my life like an axe. I had been coasting along in the oblivion of childhood when I looked up and understood that the place I had known my whole life, the only community I really knew, did not now and would not ever consider me one of them. I felt bereft. I was as much an outsider as Appletree, and much less welcome.

That night I sat in my room with the lights out, watching the snow stretch away over the fields. It was still deep cold but it hadn't snowed in over a week and the snow was starting to thin. Missy's out there, I thought. Missy's ghost. I put on my coat. I wasn't sure what I was doing, but I needed to get out. I need to put her to rest, I told myself. I barely knew what this meant; really I was just unbearably restless. *This is how she used to feel*, I thought, feeling very profound and grownup. I rounded up a few supplies: a note Missy had given me, a barrette that she'd dropped the last day of school, my Swiss army knife, a lighter. I ducked into the closet and pulled one of the stickers off the back of the shelves. I had the idea I would go down into the grove and light a little bonfire. I would burn an offering to help speed her on her way.

My parents were engrossed in *Masterpiece Theater*; it was easy to slip out the kitchen door into the night.

I went down to the wood I loved so much. The night was still, not much above zero, and the maples and beech felt thick in the dim light. For the first time the wood seemed small and confining. I wanted to be up at the top of our property, where I could see all the way to town and beyond, where the wind brought with it a taste of the river.

I passed the tree with the rope swing that Missy said her brothers had hung. I sawed off a few threads and put them in my pocket with the note and the sticker and the barrette.

I went up the track between our fields, stepping in the tire tracks Dad had made last week when he drove up to check on the neighbor's cows. *Before Missy*, I thought.

Tire tracks followed her bare feet . . . I looked over my shoulder. Dark fields and our house, still and quiet. *He chased her and pinned her up against the fence.* I pictured the headlights bearing down, the engine roaring, and Missy hyuk hyuk hyuk-ing as if this was just another of her brothers' pranks.

The wind blew right through my coat. As I approached the top of the hill from which I could see the Appletree site with its floodlights, I remembered that the man with the car was still out there. Just then an unmufflered truck turned onto the road that went past the house and I gasped and dropped to my knees, crouching until its roar faded into the night.

The car had pushed her against a fence; the barbed wire left a mark on her back. It was the same back that had lunged across my open textbook to open the window, her glittery shirt hiked up and showing the blond hair growing over the dip at the base of her spine. The same spine marked with barbed wire pin pricks. The same spine that they buried last week.

I stepped off the road in my boots and warm socks and leaned against the barbed wire so that it caught my weight. It poked into my skin through the thick fabric of my coat and I had a moment of wild panic. *This is what she felt*, I thought, *this is what it was like.* The fields, which had always felt friendly and familiar, now seemed menacing. Or worse, indifferent. It doesn't care, I realized. The land doesn't care about any of us.

I pivoted slowly, turning my back on the blazing light of Appletree Acres. There was the Miller farmhouse, a remnant of the Miller farm, which broke apart after the last remaining Miller went into a nursing home. There was the burning yard light of the family whose teenage daughter had been killed by a falling tree back when I was in kindergarten. There was the stream rumored to be radioactive due to runoff from the nuclear plant twenty miles upstream and the flat gleaming stretches of cornfields, glinting oddly in the moonlight, a strange pale brown in daylight. My dad called them nitrogen deathscapes and said his way of intensive, small-scale farming was better. I had a weary inkling that the truth was more complicated.

I suddenly felt exhausted. I took Missy's things out of my pocket and made a little pile on the icy tire track. I flicked the lighter and held it to the note, which caught the flame slowly and only burned part way. It melted part of the sticker and the barrette but nothing was burned completely. I kicked snow over the mess, feeling young and useless, and then began the long walk back, stumbling as I went.

I came across the remains of that mess last year. I had walked to the top of the hill to stretch my legs after another difficult talk with Mom and was getting ready to head back to my place across the valley. Striding along the old farm road, weedy and rutted in the years since Dad's stroke, my eye caught a dull flash in the dirt. When I knelt down I saw that it was a cheap barrette, half buried in the road. It surprised me: it was so childish, so small. I had forgotten how young Missy was when she died—barely fourteen. Younger than my kids are now. I pried it up and brushed it clean with my thumb.

The barrette was made of pink metal with a cartoonish rose at one end. I thought about how it turned out that Appletree Acres didn't kill her, after all; it was a friend of her father's, a man from a family as deep-rooted and bitter as her own. When asked why he'd been so cruel, the newspapers reported, he just shrugged. Even by then I'd stopped thinking of old farm families as being something special. Land was land, and we'd all contributed to its wreck and degradation.

I put the barrette in my pocket and kept going, down along the road until the gate, which I unlatched with the authority of a local: it was intended to block the swarms of kids and pot-shotters from the warrens of new white houses, not me. I blazed right past the Keep Out sign on the other side of the gate; Libby Trenton waved from behind her flapping laundry.

We're an old family now, in the valley; Appletree Acres began it but the changes since have ensured our place. The Mettingers sold their strip two decades ago and our road is bright with car dealerships and big box stores. I've been talking with Mom about selling, and just in the past few months she's begun to not say no. I tried to talk to the Heritage Farms Foundation, but they say our farm is too small, too surrounded, to fit their conservation strategy. There's a buyer down from Columbus who's interested, and with that money we could afford to put Dad in the nice home. I have spent many nights awake, weighing the pain.

I don't harbor any animosity to the Mettingers, or the Beckett family, or Appletree Acres. Progress, say the locals, but I disagree there, too. My dad would have said density, concentration, open space corridors: that's the way to accommodate growth. Maybe. Or maybe accommodation is a foolish dream.

This is how to become part of a place: survive and remember. When I stop in the new Kroger's to pick up toasted sesame oil and a decent Malbec, I know what I am walking over. I feel the changes in my bones. I remember how two men installing sewer line were killed here when the ditch they were digging collapsed. I think how, years before that, an awkward teenage girl with a few hours left to live stumbled through this field on bloody feet. I remember her laugh. And I reflect how we are all complicit, a little, in her death.

Bad

THERE'S APRIL, dead center but drifting away. Dandelion-puff hair, Clearasil-crusted jaw, mannequin frame. Look how she's dressed— the things we wore then! Fifty-dollar Gap miniskirt, knees showing, pink sweater with butterflies on it. I'm not kidding. Butterflies. We were still in that transition zone the year she was killed—half our wardrobe was chic, half teeny-bopper trash. Legwarmers. Jelly bracelets. Leather biker jackets.

A four-by-four glossy, gummed around the edges: it's the only photo I have of her, because that was the year I gave up taking pictures. Photography was a false art, I told April. The only reality it could capture was a superficial one, which anyone could manipulate. "Jenny," she said, "one of these days reality is going to sweep you and your little virginal self right off the face of the planet."

We lived in the subdivision with the streets named after girls. My house was on Tammy Lane and from my bedroom I could see the front door of the house on Pamela Court where April lived with her dad. Beyond her house was a ragged hedgerow and beyond that cornfields, straight to the horizon. We decided in eighth grade that we were bound for better things than suburban Ohio, humidity and honey locust trees. All good things in life scare you at first, we agreed.

"You've got to feel something *here*. Then you know you've changed," April said, laying her hand across the zipper of her jeans.

We were sitting in my parents' hand-hewn deck chairs, drinking tequila and limes from orange-juice glasses. It was the first time in my life I'd drunk anything stronger than beer. I'd felt my belly plunge when I poured it out, then again when I ran tap water into the bottle to bring the liquid back up to the level of the red T on the label, and I hoped that plunge was the feeling April was talking about. She was new in town, pudgy and mysterious, different from all my other friends. The ones who blushed in horror when I said "shit," which I did, often and loudly, although it never gave me the satisfaction I thought it should.

Starting that day April and I would be called best friends, her short and me tall, her blond and me dark, and just getting used to our new heaviness, to the way men followed us now, with their eyes. The tequila made my nose itch and I kept rubbing it, smelling the lime on my fingertips.

"It's like, you can do something, but it doesn't really affect you," I answered her, nodding. "You're doing these things on the surface, sneaking a cigarette—"

"Doing shots of tequila," she broke in, beginning to go off on a tangent. A habit of hers, I was beginning to realize. I brought the conversation deftly back to task the way my professor parents did at the dinner table.

"—*the point* is behind it you're always aware of how you're the same. Here I am, Jenny Mulligan, getting drunk. The same as Jenny Mulligan playing the oboe."

"We've got to go deeper. Deep." She giggled. The light had begun to seem brighter, slanted, and I giggled too. It came from my bottom ribs, that giggle, and I could tell without even looking at her that April's came from the same place.

"Doesn't it seem like the light's coming from the garden?" I asked, pointing toward my mom's riot of cosmos and sunflowers. I loved those flowers, wildly, the same way I loved my parents, clumsy loves I'd started trying to hide. But the way the light came down now made it okay, and April jumped up, throwing her arms wide, her chest jostling.

"It's the center of the universe!" she cried. "Right here! We're reaching out and out and out from it, to everything that's out there."

"Right here!" I echoed, and threw myself into the grass, my arms lifting into the bottomless blue sky. The smell of mud under the grass roots, my shoulders pressing into earth, sun bathing my fingers and deep inside a flickering feeling I thought was happiness. "I'm feeling it," I shouted at the sky. "This is it, April, isn't it?"

She dropped into the grass too, and said, her voice weird and close against the ground, "It's the beginning."

That was the year we started saying "bad." What we called things if they made us come in for a closer look: *That's bad*. First it was talking to people, anybody. We'd go uptown on a Friday night and dare each other: I bet you won't go talk to *them*. The high school kids who spiked their hair. The rednecks standing around their pickups spitting quick streams of brown juice. College guys. The man who sat in Burger King, counting sugar packets and muttering about narcs. "Oh, Jenny Mulligan," she'd whisper in delight when we were alone again, "you're so *bad*. I can't *believe* you asked that guy if his mother chewed tobacco too." Or I'd say it as we browsed through Looney Tunes's Used Records, bringing over an album cover to show her. "Now, this girl is bad," I'd explain, pointing to the picture of a tough-eyed woman driving a Harley, her hair streaming out behind her like a flag. Bad was being a little rude, sometimes. Bad was not worrying about being safe. Women like the one on the Harley weren't simply free, we agreed: they were in touch with something that other people just didn't get.

In high school it got harder. I dyed my hair blue; she pierced her nose. We shoplifted. There was the sense of a line that needed to be crossed. We showed up at parties, got high for the first time, watched other kids make out. "This is bullshit," April said once as we walked home, the party sounds growing smaller behind us. "The night is alive! Smell it! The flowers!" She dragged herself along a lilac bush. "And the only choices open to us are getting blitzed and clawing at some idiot in a letter jacket."

The summer before our sophomore year I drove us down to Cincinnati without even a learner's permit to drive. "Oh, Jenny," she shouted, leaning her whole body out the window into the humid night, "this is fucking awesome!" We drove the back way, along the river, where the fireflies were as thick as stars. All I can remember of that night is my anxiety, imagining my parents coming back from the Mostly Mozart Festival and finding me gone. I had told them I was sick. "Don't be such a prude," April said, cranking around the rearview mirror so she could adjust her lipstick. No, I corrected her, a prude was someone who was afraid to show her slip in public. "Doesn't sound wrong to me," she said. I drove on, my stomach clenching and unclenching.

This is what bad girls do, I tried to convince myself later, grounded for two weeks, my mind wandering as I practiced oboe scales over and over again. We don't give a soaring shit. ("Jenny, your tone is slipping at the top," called my mother from the kitchen. She and my dad had been shocked into speechlessness by our adventure.) I tried to ignore the tiny voice that said: but you give a shit what *April* thinks.

It was while I was grounded that April met Jason. "He's a photographer," she told me, dragging me to Ozzie's Grill to meet him. "Experimental stuff, really cool, like posed shots. You're going to love him."

"Is he a senior?" was all I could think of to ask. Neither of us had had a boyfriend before and I didn't know the protocol. I felt stupid, virginal.

"No, dork, I told you before. He's in college. An art major. But he's taking time off." She laughed her new laugh, a throaty, fakey sound that set my teeth on edge.

She marched us back to the kitchen, right past the college girl waitresses who watched us with a kind of grim pity. April didn't notice them because she was already squeezing one of the cooks, a guy with skin the color of his apron, with a doughy belly and enormous feet squeezed into high-heeled vinyl boots. "Here's my new man," she said. And who was your old man, I wanted to say.

He wouldn't look at me right away but kept buttering pans. It was like he was shy, or busy, and April had to stroke him under the chin with a finger. "Meet my best friend, honey," she purred.

So he dropped the pan, finally, and flicked his eyes over me. The lashes were long and silky and fluttered over his swollen cheeks. "She looks like Debbie fucking Gibson," he said.

"Oh, meanie, be nice," April said, but giggled. My cheeks burned and I made myself watch as she squished her breasts into his back and then made out with him, her lipstick smearing onto his face. This is bad, I told myself, this is deep, even though what it seemed like was exactly what every other girl about to start tenth grade was doing. Clawing some idiot in a letter jacket.

"What do you see in him?" I asked after the manager cook made us leave.

"Oh, he's standoffish at first," April said, lighting a cigarette. "But he has this scared little boy inside. His art is all really deep, babies in barbed wire and bruised faces and patterns, like the inner emotions of everyday objects."

"Oh," I said. Later that night I yelled at my baby sister, a snarl that made her bawl and got me grounded again. I kicked my bed, weeping.

· · ·

The first day of sophomore year April met me at the bus stop, out of breath. "Check it out!" she said, flipping up her shirt and pushing down the top of her jeans. There was some black spidery writing there; when I looked closely, I saw it was his name. Jason K.

"You let him tattoo you?" I asked, breaking out into a sweat.

"The pain is like this high," she said. "At first I can't stand it but then it reaches this point where it's like overload and then I'm in this other dimension. It's so awesome." Her whole face shone, eyes, teeth, lipstick. I felt jealousy like a pinch at my side. Nothing I'd ever done had seemed this great to her.

"What are you going to do when you guys break up?" I said. She shook her head, the blond kinks bouncing back and forth. They were never breaking up, she told me.

She brought a stack of his photos to geometry class. They were dark-room-developed pictures, almost as large as the special notebook she kept them in. There was a picture of a naked figure groping the bars of a bamboo cage; another of the university duck pond that made it look like a brooding eye. These are good, I thought, stunned. That week, alone—April's father was out of town and April, supposedly with me, spent every afternoon and evening at Jason's apartment—I wandered around town with my Kmart camera, snapping pictures. Buildings, trees, trash, people. I used up three rolls of film and when they came back they were oddly disappointing. Just a stack of three-by-five snapshots, nothing about them shocking or startling. They looked like extra photos from the yearbook archives. One of them was the one I still have of April; there was nothing in it of her craziness, her energy. Nothing of *her*. She just looked like any other girl.

October. The leaves blazed red and fell and I was seeing April only once, twice a week outside of school. She said my family made her itchy: "All that good for you stuff they always do." Her nose wrinkled and she fingered the sore that had risen on her upper lip. So we spent the time at her house, smoking dope she'd borrowed from Jason, looking through her dad's art books. He had a new book on his table, *Andrew Wyeth: The Helga Pictures*. I couldn't stop turning the pages, staring at this ethereal woman with the mannish face. She looked like she was beyond bad and deep, I thought. Her naked body, middle-aged, stretched out pale and vulnerable, page after page.

"Model, muse," April said. "Like what I am to Jason."

"What do you mean?" I tried to picture what they might do together and all I could come up with was her sitting in a chair, straight and uncomfortable, like she was having her school portrait done. I couldn't imagine her in any of the Helga poses.

"Oh, you know. We've been trying new things. No more static stills. Landscape art, moving, encountering. It's so deep, so raw, really cool." Her voice so bland it was like she was telling me they played Scrabble.

"Like what?" I said.

"You know. Just deep stuff. He's this genius, I think, and his stuff just, it gets me. Way down here. I'm all inside-out."

I tried to imagine where "here" was, what "inside-out" meant. I was sure by then that I wasn't as deep as April, that she'd go places I wouldn't go, and what she said made a cold wind blow across my heart. *I* wanted to be somebody's muse.

"You couldn't do this with photographs," I said then. I don't know why I said that. "This spirit in them," I went on, "like the way she seems to breathe. Photographs just show a superficial reality."

April glanced at the book. "Jason says artists like Andrew Wyeth are wannabee photographers. He says if you're going to paint realistically you should just take a picture. Photographers take the world as it is and make it into what they want. Painters have to make stuff up. They try too hard."

"If you want to catch somebody's spirit, somebody's soul"—this was when I could still use the word soul—"you've got to paint them," I answered. "Photos are just blips, slices, not real."

She shrugged. "Whatever 'reality' is, Jenny."

. . .

I stole the *Helga* book and stared at the pictures all weekend, posing myself in front of my bedroom mirror. My body was a washout, like Debbie-fucking-Gibson, limp blue hair growing out brown, knees square, breasts small and pale, like mole heads. Face scabby and, my mother always said, sensible. Someone who tries too hard. I stood there naked until I got cold, trying to make what I saw into something eerie and sensuous, like Helga. Or April. This is like sub-reality, I thought. Suburban reality. Somewhere else is the real stuff, deep down. Bad. *Raw*.

I got my driver's license in November, the same week Jason was fired from Ozzie's. April started spending all her afterschool time at his place, a room in a residential motel out on US 27. The Coachlight Motel. It smelled of mice and Cheetos.

I'd start driving and find myself there, bored, lonely. They would come out into the day, blinking, and I'd feel like a tourist. Neither of them would really look at me. April had started to look grubby.

I hung out with the two of them sometimes. I kept wanting Jason to notice me, to see that I was just as deep as April, but his eyes when he glanced my way were cold and uninterested. Just before Thanksgiving we were sitting on his broken-down couch, smoking and throwing the butts out the open door into the gravel, trying to hit the patch of dead grass to see if it would catch fire.

"April tells me you don't believe in photography," Jason said, turning to stare right at me.

"Just snapshots, all that tourist stuff, not real photography. You know what I mean," I said quickly.

"Snapshots aren't real?" He leaned forward, pretending to be puzzled.

"I mean they're real, just not, you know, thought-out."

"So how do you make this distinction between art and junk?"

I glanced at April for help but she was mooning up at Jason, her expression eager, even anxious. Whenever she moved I could see her chest jiggle underneath her shirt and I thought I sensed a strange smell coming off her hair.

"Well, you know, it's how much it's thought-out, if it's just another picture by the 'Welcome to Yellowstone' sign or whatever or if it's trying to make a statement, be something unique, you know." I felt panicky.

"So who determines this 'uniqueness quotient'? Is it you?" He caught April's eye and she simpered.

"Do you think they've ever had water in that pool?" I said. I hadn't noticed it until this second, a little ten-by-twelve cavity with flaking blue paint on the inside.

"The real question is, do you think you can just dismiss us like that? I asked you a question."

"Shut up, Jason," April said suddenly. "You're scaring her." I thought she was rescuing me and I actually smiled, grateful, but she didn't notice. Her face was worried, adult.

"Shut up? Shut up? Don't tell me to shut up." He shifted around, pushed her off his lap.

"I'll tell you what I want." She held herself rigid, arms folded, staring straight ahead.

"You know what I can do." He glanced at me, then out at the guys working on a car across the way.

"I know what you can do." Neither of them spoke after that. I finished my cigarette and left, my belly tight. Jason is such an asshole, I told myself, the word punching into my mouth like I was understanding it for the first time. And April just went right along with him, like she had no mind of her own.

Maybe April's an asshole, too, that tiny voice in my head whispered. Sly as snakes.

How much did I guess, then, of what was going on between them? It came out in Jason's trial the way he'd make her do things, or get her to do things, film her doing gymnastics naked in the park, doing things with kitchenware, with animals. The stuff they accused him of has come back to me years later at three, four in the morning and I try to imagine April going through with it, laughing that fakey, throaty laugh. They wouldn't show the videotapes in court so I don't know if she was smiling when she did these things, laughing, another big joke, if she was shaking, or if she had that tense, angry set to her jaw that she would get sometimes when I asked her *but what happened.*

The first snow came early that year, before December. It was only a dusting on the frozen mud but I felt elated anyway, when I woke up to it. It was as though the long dry fall had allowed things to get out of control, and here was winter, to bring them back to normal. I dressed slowly in the whitened light and drank two cups of coffee. Talawanda School District Plan B, said the radio. School wouldn't start until ten. My homework was all done so I got out my sketchbook and drew: the coffee cup, my little sister watching her turtle, my mom grading her students' papers. I tried to get both her annoying cheerfulness and the way she sighed sometimes as she worked, pressing her lips together and adjusting her glasses, as if life wasn't working out the way she'd wanted.

This is reality, I argued April in my head as I drew. Not your stupid boyfriend and his posed pictures; who needs you? I pressed the soft tip harder into the paper to drown out the voice that answered, *you're just trying your little heart out, aren't you?* Today would be the day I'd call up Erin Rawlins from band, I decided. See if she wanted to do something.

I jumped when the phone rang. It was April. We hadn't talked on the phone in over a month and I tried to keep the choke of excitement out of my voice.

Her voice sounded different; split-open, maybe. Wheedling. "Hey, girl," she said. "What's going down?"

It didn't take her long to get to her real purpose, which was she wanted a ride out to Jason's. "Okay," I said.

You're a real sucker, I told myself when I hung up the phone.

By the time I got over to April's I had decided that I'd give her a ride but this would be the last of it, the last time I did anything with her. The absolute last time. I pulled into her driveway and honked the horn once, angrily.

When she came out I asked her why she didn't have her dad ferry her around. She pushed a big pink duffle bag into the back seat and didn't say anything, no smart remarks, no snappy comeback. I looked at her then. She was wearing sunglasses and seemed heavier, somehow, or slower, like she'd been put into the wrong body.

"What's going on?" I said, pulling out of the drive. "Is your dad mad or something?"

She shrugged.

"You can't just expect me to drive you around," I said.

"I know."

The roads were slick at all of the stop signs, so I had to drive carefully, both hands on the wheel, my eyes on the road.

"I'm sick of this. We're supposed to be best friends."

She picked at something on her fingernail and shrugged again.

"You never tell me anything anymore!"

"It's not like that. There's nothing to tell."

"It's not like what? *What's* not to tell?" At the edge of the subdivision I turned west, into farmland, instead of toward town. April lifted her head then, and her shoulders froze, but she didn't say anything. We drove out through frozen cornfields.

"I don't know anything about you," I said. "You're like this stranger sitting there."

She shifted, and an odor of mice and incense settled out of her poncho. I thought I saw the corner of her lip curling like a smile.

"It's not like that. Not most of the time. I—we—go places you couldn't even imagine."

"Like what? When is it 'like that'?"

There was a stop sign, way out in the middle of the cornfields, and I had to stop at it, the sound of the car dying down to the whir of the heater. April waited until the engine was loud again before she said,

"Oh, you know, he has his bad days. Or I think it's my bad days, my resistance."

"*Bad*," I said. I meant it lightly, as in: Remember the goofy things we used to say? But the words stuck in the air, heavy as stone. April sighed and looked out the window.

She didn't care anymore about what we used to call things. That was obvious. She was off in her own planet of badness, and stupid old Jenny was left behind with the rest of the prudes. I wished I could pinch her.

I look back at those two sixteen-year-olds in the battered old Volvo and I can still smell my misery, the loneliness that seeped into my mind like poison. Did I really not know what she was saying to me? At the time all I could hear was the pride in her voice, the scorn: you could never do this, Jenny. And that scorn made me cruel; at least, that's how I explained it to myself, afterward.

It was the week after that she showed up on my doorstep. Her hair was clean and soft again and she wasn't wearing makeup, which made her look older, more experienced. More like Helga. Don't say anything, I told myself, but let her in. We each got a big stack of cookies and a glass of milk and went up to my room to look through the sketchbook from my college art class, the one where we drew live nudes. I showed her the painting I'd done of her house, the one that made it look like a face, dark and sad, with the juniper bushes growing over its front windows and the field of broken cornstalks behind it. She glanced over everything too quickly, preoccupied.

"I've decided," she said abruptly. "It just isn't working out anymore."

I remember it as coming out of the blue like that. "What isn't working anymore?" I asked, my hand pausing mid-turn. Hoping.

"He's just too much of a genius. It gets old. I *want* things. Is that so wrong?"

I shook my head.

"I mean, it's like give me a fucking break. I mean, I love him, whatever he thinks, and I love his art, it's amazing, but I'm sixteen, you know?

I'm too young for all this heavy shit he pours on. You're right, Jenny. I should be sensible like you."

She'd only eaten half a cookie and she sat back on her heels. "I mean, he's not going to like this, not at *all*. But screw him, right? I'm just going to have to take a deep breath and do it."

I just watched her, my hand still frozen, a smile beginning to creep up toward my lips. I tried to think of something sensible to say.

"You've got to stand up for yourself," I said, finally.

"Oh, *thank* you. That is so true. That is so so so so true. That's what everyone says."

She talked for a half an hour, her eyes wild, searching the corners of my ceiling.

"So what are you waiting for," I finally said. "Let's go out there." I could feel the old dizzy excitement as the words came out of my mouth. "He's such an asshole, April. You've got to end it now." I heard the confidence in my voice and thought, this is it. I'm taking action. No more Jenny-on-the-sidelines for me.

"He's not going to like it," she said, as if waiting for me to say what I said next:

"So who the fuck cares? This is your thing, April. This is your life."

She nodded, pulling her hair down over her ears. I offered to drive—I could hardly believe she'd let me be there—but she nodded again, barely noticing.

"I can't believe I don't even have a fucking license to drive," was all she said. "What a waste, huh?"

We hugged, quickly. Her hair smelled of lavender shampoo but under that lingered the mouse smell and something else.

After she'd left I threw out the cookies she hadn't eaten and poured the milk down the bathroom sink. Outside there were kids running up and down the street in bright quilted coats, pink and blue and yellow. They don't have any idea what's coming to them, I thought, feeling old and dangerous. If they even knew what just transpired behind this window . . . I imagined them watching me, solemn and impressed.

· · ·

We drove over the next day, after school. Two or three times on the drive over April said, matter-of-factly, "Just let me do the talking. He can be weird. All I want you to do is give me a little moral support." I nodded, thinking *well, duh*, and trying to think of what I'd say when it was all over.

As we waited at the stoplight at US 27—my turning signal clicking away—April stirred slightly and said, "Maybe this isn't such a good idea. Having you come too. Maybe you should just drop me off."

It felt like a slap. Even then I didn't think she meant it the way I took it. On some level I knew she wasn't trying to leave me behind, which is probably why I said, stoically, "We've just got to go through with it. Like ripping off a band aid." But my hands gripped the steering wheel harder, as in, *Just try to pry me off.* And inside I distinctly thought, *you can't just take this away from me. It isn't right.*

I was going to see for myself what bad was, if it killed me. Bad and deep and raw. I was going to be there, no matter what she said.

I pulled into the motel parking lot and parked in the center, on the patch of weeds under the sign saying "Coachlight Motel—Weekly and Monthly Rates Aval." Jason's door opened and I gripped the steering wheel, feeling my skin stick to the grubby vinyl. This is it, I told myself.

Jason glanced toward us with his half-closed eyes and glanced away, up toward the sky. I wondered if he knew why we were there, or if he thought I was just dropping her off as usual. Here's Debbie-fucking-Gibson, I imagined saying to him. In your face, asshole. I wondered if I'd be able to keep my nerve.

I let April get out of the car first. The door let out a huge creak and Jason looked our way, as if he'd just noticed us. He started walking over, huge against the sky. I'm feeling it here, I wanted to whisper to April, but didn't want to spoil the mood. We arranged ourselves against the front bumper of my car, not quite brushing hips. Jason had stopped about ten feet off, as if he knew what was coming, and April leaned forward and said, "Like I promised, Jason. I'm telling you in person."

When he didn't say anything, just looked at her, silent and sort of dense, she went on, "This is it. I can't do this anymore. We've got to take a break." She pitched her voice a little louder than normal, as if he were hard of hearing.

Jason just stood there, tapping one finger against his palm. She gave me an apologetic look, although I wasn't sure if she was apologizing to me or to him. "It's too much," she said again. "I can't do this anymore."

Finally he spoke. "Who's going to get my tattoos?" he said. His voice was wheezy and awful. April didn't answer.

He stepped closer. "Didja hear me?" he said. "Who's going to get all my beautiful tattoos? My artwork. My stuff. You know?"

He looked at me as he said that, dragging out the syllables in a harsh lisping croon: be-*yoo*-tiful dat-*toos*; and it came to me with total clarity that this was the moment to act. I watched myself in amazement as I stepped toward him and made the nastiest, prissiest face I could. "So what are you going to do?" I asked him. "You going to make us give them up?"

"What if," he said, still low and lisping. "What if I am?" He put his big ugly paw over April's arm and starting rubbing. He had this smug smile, like he knew he was going to get away with whatever he wanted. Asshole, I thought, but couldn't quite say.

"Push around a couple of girls," April said. "That's real macho." Her eyes avoided his face as she said this, and her voice, while sarcastic, was low. A mumble. Speak up! I wanted to say.

He took her face in a rough pinch.

"Oh, yeah," I said, echoing her sarcasm and turning it up a notch. "You're a stud!" Even as I said it I was cheering inside: I'm standing up for April! I'm doing it! Not to say my voice didn't stutter and stretch, my mouth weirdly misshapen by something which might have been terror. Or exhilaration.

April kind of jerked her head toward me, eyes wide, her face still pinched toward Jason, but all I could see suddenly were Jason's eyes, now fixed on me, burning, the skin around them like metal.

"What?" he said, leering over at me. "What'd you say?"

Again the misshapen mouth, the words refusing to form just right. "I said, go screw yourself, you big asshole!" I burst out at last. "We're sick of you!"

It wasn't quite the rousing speech I had hoped for but I still felt like I was running, even flying, into the thick of the battle and maybe winning, or at least keeping up. We're doing it, I wanted to say to April, but I didn't have time, because Jason grabbed my arm, right below the elbow, and half lifted me so that I had to struggle to keep my elbow from bending the wrong way.

"You're just a little freaky bitch, aren't you?" he said, shaking me, and I felt the way I did when I was in second grade and the fifth graders would pin me to the wall and whisper in my ear, "Tell us you stink. Say it. Say, 'I stink,'" and there would be no way to wriggle out and I'd be forced to say it, crying.

"I'm not," I was about to say, when April spoke instead, her voice heavy. With disgust, I thought, or pity.

"Jesus, Jason," she said. "Get off her already. You're such a loser."

He dropped my arm and I fell down so hard I could feel the bruise starting up.

"Don't fuck with me," Jason said, his voice still soft. "I'm just getting tired of you fucking with me."

"I'm not fucking with you," she said. "This is just it. Just figure it out. This is it."

God she's brave, I thought, staring at her. She stood with her head down, her hands in her pockets, the pink marks of his horrible hand still on her cheeks. I thought her stillness was calmness. And even that I wanted in on. I couldn't rest until I'd pushed myself in to wherever she was, stood beside her to face the fire; so I put my hands in my pockets, too, squeezing them into fists, and felt just a fraction closer to calm.

"It, huh? It?" Jason's eyes started to bug out, and his face turned white, then red, then white, and then he made a lunge at her, like he was going to smash her flat; instead he reared up a huge booted leg and kicked the front grill of my car, smashing a jagged hole in it. I gasped, my calmness blasted away.

He kicked it again, and again, his nostrils flaring and his top lip tight against his teeth. My whole car bounced up and down with each kick. I stood frozen, like a pantomime of a scream. Look what he's doing! I shrieked to myself, as if I could stop looking.

Halfway through a kick he whirled around and started to storm away, swearing to himself. He grabbed a fistful of his own hair and yanked it, and his face crumpled as though he was about to cry. Then he kicked the dirt, whirled around, and came back. "You know what I think," he said. "You know what I think. You say I'm a loser but would a loser do this?"

His hand came out of his pocket and I saw the knife in it, the little knife that seemed too small to do any real harm. I remember seeing it and thinking, oh, that? And I've always said it was relief that kept me from shouting, "Look out!"—but even then I thought it might be something else. The way the knife seemed like the next logical step, the next unfolding moment of this crazy story I was finally caught up in, a part of—and I *wanted* that moment. You know? How you can wish an event into being?

He grabbed April up and hit her on the neck, a deep soft thumping sound. He pulled back, surprised, and she just stood there, didn't retort anything, didn't say a word; her hand was at her neck and her eyes were wide in disbelief. Jason nodded at her, a short sharp jerk of his head, confirming. Then she dropped to her knees in the gravel so hard I winced. I reached out to her, already starting to gabble itsokay itsokay itsokay. "Don't pass out," I shrieked. "Just don't pass out on me!" The words felt fake in my mouth, and she made a sound like she was trying to swallow but couldn't.

Jason dropped the knife and disappeared. In the second between dropping the knife and running away, he caught my eye, and for the first time he looked at me with something other than annoyed indifference. I've tried to figure that look out. His face was flushed, his mouth close to a smile, and so it was almost like we were sharing a joke. But as he ran off he made a sound like a moan or a sob. Later they arrested him on the railroad tracks, less than a mile from the Coachlight Motel, as though he'd tried to run away but lost the heart for it.

April sank in on herself, losing blood, her face going frightened, then indifferent, then gray. I stayed with her until the ambulance came, holding my hand to the hole in her neck; when they pried me away I was covered with her blood and still saying, "Don't do this, April, don't don't don't."

I was the hero, right? That's how everyone treated me, from then on. But I knew better. I knew that if I'd been a better friend that day, a better person, April would still be alive, and that knowledge wormed its way into me like a little barbed fishhook.

At the end of that endless day she died, after everything had been said and written down and I had been squinted at, questioned, washed, I stepped into my own room from the hallway. My hair was wet and I wore only a T-shirt. The room was dark except for the orange shapes made by the streetlight on the headboard of my bed. I let myself lie down, so that I was on my back, staring at the dingy corner of the ceiling where paint drips overlapped and hardened, catching dust.

My body stretched flat on the bed, bent at the knees, my toes brushing the floor. Leg bones, pelvic girdle, spine, ribs, organs, shoulder blades, arm bones, neck, skull. I could even follow the blood as it pushed through my soft and flawless veins. Everything neat and clean and working properly, but empty. *One of these days reality is going to sweep you and your little virginal self right off the face of the planet.* And lo, so it came to pass.

I'd wanted to be bad so much. I thought it would make me deeper, cooler, freer; I thought it was the way to shake off my boring, sensible self once and for all. I didn't understand what April was telling me, which was this: it's the easiest thing in the world to stop being good and, once you stop, you can never go back.

Burning

WE WOKE THAT night to the dogs barking like it was the end of the world, and to hear the mushheads at the office tell it, it was. The boys sent away, Henry transferred to Idaho, me back in my own apartment, alone again. But it's been an eon and half since I paid them any mind. I'm up on the mesa with the best of them, old firefighter Ray, and though last fall's entire disaster is spread out below me—the angry swath where the Dago Bird Refuge used to be, the Forest Service compound with its tiny American flag, the three burnt hulks of the snowplows Henry and I are still paying for—I'm cool with it. I can feel the coolness within me like a potable spring.

Then the radio in my breast pocket gives a staticky, "Ten-four, Nancy, let's get her started," and I turn around and blast the underside of the nearest oakbrush with a ribbon of flame. At first it just shrivels the leaves and blackens the bark, but pretty soon a crack of molten orange opens up. I wait until I've made sure it's going to catch and then I walk down the road, counting my paces, fifty yards until the next blast of flame. I look back up at my first one and it's smudging nicely, not too hot but a good slow smolder that should take all morning to work its way uphill. It's the middle of March and a perfect day for burning, overcast and still. God, it's good to get out of the office. I take a deep breath and swing back my hair.

I blast and scan, tracing where the fire will eat through the choking green, from the road up to the chalk cliffs where Ray and I have cut our fireline. All oakbrush. Once we've burned this slope over the deer will come back, the hawks will hunt here again, and I'm thinking maybe, if we're lucky, we'll get Lewis's woodpeckers. At the office we emphasize the practical aspect of prescribed burns. Less fuel, less chance of catastrophic fire, Ray will say, laying his hands palm down on the Formica conference table. Only once the district ranger's nodding will I add the bit about the wildlife. "These systems need fire," I finish, "to clean them out." I do not say, to let them breathe: too spiritual for this crowd.

Plus it's just a hair too close. They'd get it. They'd make the leap. Brush, family, overgrowth, fire. Renewal. And the pity would be back, unbearable, unbalancing. How can I put this so they believe me? Four years ago, it was me, my dog Bette, and my truck; now it's me, Bette, my truck, and a decent apartment. In the middle there was—what? One mess after another.

Ray's firing his way up toward where I am. He's got his ponytail tucked into the collar of his shirt and even from here I can tell he is frowning with concentration, looking each oakbrush up and down for the best spot to aim his torch. Ray's a good guy. He's the only one at the office that hasn't come at me with his false concern, his voice hushed with the Gravity of it all, hasn't tried to corner me behind some closed door so I can Tell Him What I Really Feel. Maybe that's because Ray, with his wife Rita, was our friend from before; maybe it's just his way: gentle and discreet (the polar opposite of me). I don't know and I don't ask.

He moves slower than I do, scientific and cautious, still getting used to this idea of fire as good. We've been the prescribed burn team for two years and he's more serious about it now than I am, I think. He's always photocopying articles from the *Fire Management Journal* and leaving them on my desk. But under the precision and the pondering he's got a firefighter's heart, big and red and tender to the slightest curl of smoke. Destruction makes him nervous.

I, on the other hand, love fire, the way it's almost alive, the way it transforms everything. Take anything from around me now and notice how it feeds my excitement. The stench of the propane, the weight of the torch at the end of my arm, its blackened nozzle, even my cracked and burnished work gloves. I send a blast of flame shooting up over my head, burning a juniper from the top down, just the way they tell you not to. I squat to light a huge dry branch lying in the road, then heave it up into the brush, a little advance sortie. The motion almost blows it out, and I hold my breath until I see the flame creep back, curling over the top of the stick and spilling out into the dry leaves around it.

Henry used to accuse me of preferring fire to people, specifically such people as him and the boys. He used to say if I had my way I'd live in an efficiency apartment with one of every bare necessity, one knife, one fork, one pair of underwear, all neatly lined up in the closet. I told him if I had one pair of underwear I'd be wearing it. But secretly we both knew he was right, and I even thought about those spats as I signed the lease this winter, and had to smile. Whatever else, Henry certainly knew me. Without him and the boys, my life is clean and simple. I get home, roam the hills with Bette until dark, and then we both have our kibble and bits and straighten ourselves for the following day. My boots have never been so well polished, my gear never in better repair, and I even have time to brush Bette's teeth with an old toothbrush and a little baking soda, the way she likes.

· · ·

As I burn my mind can drift back. There's no territory too dangerous when I've got a propane torch in my hand, you could say, or maybe it's the weather, moody and quiet, and no one crowding in on me. I'm like Janis Joplin, gargantuan beside Henry, who looked like he just finished riding the Preakness. The boys were both rodeo heartthrobs, cherubic blonds with brown eyes. We once made the mistake of having a family studio portrait done and we could never bring ourselves to hang it up, it's that unnerving. I called it the Manson Family Rides Again. Henry took it down to his desk and managed to lose it within a month. And the photo didn't even hint at the squabbles we had. Face it, I find myself telling an imaginary audience, some families are better off apart.

Evan, fourteen, and Chris, ten. Early on I asked Henry about their mother. "Up and left one day," he said. "Wanted nothing to do with them or me." That was all. His disgust told me everything I needed to know, I thought, and I took it as a warning. I couldn't even tell you now what I thought I'd been warned against. But I kept my distance, mostly. My job was to make jokes, keep things light. I let Henry be the parent and I was more like the laughing godmother. The godmother who slept with their dad, of course.

Take that time Evan spray painted naked women on the back of the Forest Service office building. Almost a year ago. It's not a capital crime, is what I said. And they were interesting naked women, some skinny, some fat, some wearing Coco Chanel hats and carrying pocketbooks. They're kinda cute, I told Henry. He refused to laugh. I told him the office needed new paint anyway, and he said I was missing the point. "Oh, Hanky, what is the point," I groaned, and he said, "The point is, you've got to take things seriously some of the time. This is bigger than a stupid wall. This is his life. This is *our* life. Sometimes I may not want to take it seriously either but I have to, that's my job. Get it?" And there was a moment there that we stared each other down, for a long minute seeing each other the way everyone else sees us, until I caught the twitch under his mustache and reached out to tweak his skinny little belly. Chris came in, then, sidling up between us the way he always did when our fights were over, and I assumed that was the end of it.

. . .

This is what I love about the field: there's nothing right now but the sound of boots on gravel and the hiss of my propane tank. I continue down the hill, the walking a sort of meditation. My mind wanders, my eyes wander. I can't see the CDOT burn or the Forest Service compound anymore, so instead I look wide, twenty miles across the river to the opaque shadows of Nipple Peak and beyond. It's raining over there, or snowing, even. Good. A heavy, windless rain is what we need this afternoon.

So far, so good. All Ray and I have talked about today is logistics. When I come to the end of my line I sit on the truck bumper and watch him, the way he lifts up the edges of the underbrush delicately, really thinking before he points his flame. He sets his feet down the same way, avoiding ruts and rocks. Slow, steady, focused but oblivious. Is this fondness I'm feeling? I ask myself for amusement's sake, but I have to think about it. Is that what this odd lightness across my shoulders is called? Or is it merely relief, at being out of the office? For all that I can tell a good story I'm the village idiot when it comes to feelings, and I guess that's one of the things I always liked about Henry: he knew his. Anger, horniness, corniness, love. And he knew I had mine under the crazy stories and the smartass jokes. I got used to him reading me before I did, and it throws me, now, to have to come up with the terminology on my own. Not that anyone's seriously trying, that presumptuous prying at the office aside. I shift one of my boots on the gravel, its weight dragging the rest of my leg along.

Ray comes up to me, saying, "She's looking good. Firing well. And this cloud cover ought to keep her in check."

I agree. This is the sort of material my conversations are made of, these days. The conversations I allow, at least. No more agonizing over whether to ground Evan *again* or try to figure out something more creative. No more arguing about whether study hall is a class and whether it's morally if not legally okay to skip it. No more pointless wondering if Henry and I can have something together that isn't about the boys.

Ray and I stand twenty feet apart or so, facing up the oakbrush slope that is starting to catch and smolder, the smoke drifting down and settling into our clothes and hair. I'm about to say something smartass when Ray speaks instead.

"We're getting some elk burgers and the last of the apricot preserves out this weekend. Clean out the pantry and the freezer before the summer gets going. Rita said to ask you. Our treat."

My heart sinks and I wish I didn't have to answer. "I was sort of thinking of heading over to Denver this weekend," I lie. "Visit my sister, shop some."

Ray pokes his head forward with approval. "Keep up with the family, yes," he says. "The two of you are close, I remember. Got to hold onto that."

We're not close, my sister and I. We bore each other.

"Yeah, family. What a joy," I mutter, throwing my gear into the back of the truck. It's time to start for the top of the burn, to make sure we keep the damage under control. I hear Ray clear his throat behind me and I throw my gear in the truck and start it up, rev the gas over anything he might be saying.

He waits until we're driving to continue. "How're things going, then?"

This is not, not, not a conversation I want to have, at this particular moment. At any particular moment. "Oh, fine," I answer. "Really, fine."

I drive fast, up past where we've been torching all morning, gunning into the soft mud in the shadow of the roadcut, slipping a little, pulling free. I tell myself he needed to say his little piece, to get it out, and now he'll let it go. I hope this, anyhow, but suspect he's still chewing on something over there because he keeps making these fake coughs and fluffing himself.

Coming up is the part of the road we talk about in safety meetings, where it narrows to the width of a pickup and erosion has eaten it away on the drop-off side. If he were to look out his window now, Ray could see two hundred feet down to the remains of the last truck that took this curve too fast. Ray's got his eyes straight ahead. We're supposed to take this section at a crawl but I don't brake. I steer into the bank, not so much that we bounce off it but enough to lift the tires on the driver's side and tilt us more sharply toward the cliffs. I see a rut edge that will keep us level if I catch it just right. I don't so much steer as finesse the wheel, smoothing my hand across it like I'm flattening a bed sheet. At twenty-five miles an hour it's an impressive move, one only a few folks at the Forest Service could pull off. Only a few people would even try, and believe me, Ray may be a firefighter but he isn't one of them. I make it. I glance over at him without moving my head. I'm hoping I've shut him up, but I can't tell.

At the crest of the next switchback I turn in at the fireline we've cut. Hacked-off oakbrush branches squeal against the paint and it's loud enough in the cab that we don't have to talk anymore. I drive to the end, where the slope is in permanent shadow and still harbors snow. There's a smell here like winter, which makes me think, for no reason, of the herons. We get out and start uncoiling the hoses.

Ray goes out one way with one hose, and I go out the other, and when we've reached as far as we can in either direction we get back in the truck and drive back toward the road. It's kind of communal and quiet, just the popping of the fire as it moves our way and the hiss of water hitting leaves. We talk, but it's basic stuff: whether the wind's changing, how the sky looks, whether the rain will come like we're hoping it will.

The night herons came back this spring. I saw the first one two weeks ago, a male, poking around the charred remains of the old heronry. I squatted in the weeds for an hour watching him through my binoculars; he'd poke through the unburnt stuff, finicky, and wade along the shore where the tamarisk still shaded it. He'd fly off for a while, and then come back, and forage some more. Right at dusk he lifted his head and took off, flying in the direction of the river. They'll nest somewhere else until the preserve grows back, I guess.

"They look like puppets!" Chris said the first time I brought him out to the preserve for some birdwatching—and they do; I'd never thought of it before, but they look exactly like puppets you could pull over your forearm, just that shape and awkward and careful, the way puppets would move. The birdwatching was pretty much against my rules but we both liked it enough that I made an exception. Two or three times a month we'd pack sandwiches and head out at first light, just the two of us, never talking much except to point out birds.

The month before the fire, Chris and I had snuck up to the night heron nest and watched the chicks, two strapping healthy things with the ugliest awkwardest fuzz you could imagine. It felt a little like we were playing hooky, leaving Henry and Evan alone to sleep off their latest fight. Chris leaned in, enormous-eyed, holding his breath, plucking at my elbow. "We shouldn't touch them," he decided, and instead we stroked the reeds around the nest, dipped our fingers in the icy marshwater, gently poked the dry sticks. The chicks would clack their oversize beaks at our fingers if they strayed too close, but in between their beaks would open piteously, flashing the pattern of gape and throat. Chris pulled me away so that the adult birds could return and we watched from behind an olive thicket until our knees got cold and stiff. I pulled our sandwiches out of my pack and pulled off pieces for Chris so he could watch through the binoculars and then he did the same for me, biting off a piece and giving a piece.

I tell myself that if Ray and I end up talking about the whole Henry mess today that I am going to keep Chris out of it.

More than halfway down the fireline the drizzle begins and it's clear we won't need this extra strip of watered ground. Ray and I keep going anyway, without even having to consult each other. With him it's probably cautiousness and with me it's putting off the miserable wait in the truck as long as possible. We're committed to a long day here, until the fire's reached the fireline and been subdued, or peters out of its own accord.

I zip up my rain slicker and train the hose into the oakbrush below me. I watch the silvery spray battle the smoke-gray drizzle, the oakbrush drinking it all up greedily. This line of brush is spared the fire, for now, and I imagine it already sending runnels underground to take the space opened up by the burn. I know very well that oakbrush doesn't grow by runnels, but it spreads almost as fast and as thick as if it did. Part of me hates this part of the prescribed burns, where we have to put it out.

I'm remembering the last time we went camping with Ray and Rita, the last time we did anything as a family at all—almost a year ago now, last Memorial Day. We thought we were at some kind of truce, sitting around the fire with the other adults, talking about the summer to come, the fires that were already starting, down near Grand Junction, the seasonal crews we had coming on the following week, the way the whole summer was shaping up quick into a hectic replica of all the previous summers. The mosquitoes weren't out yet and the air was frigid as soon as the sun dropped into the trees: the adults were bundled into lawn chairs and the kids were playing some elaborate running game in untied sneakers and shorts. When the sun started streaking orange through the trees we called them in for bratwursts and potato salad, and Rita made everyone in her family wash their hands before eating, even Ray, who looked at us sheepishly.

"She's got him whupped," Henry said to me later, in the tent, both of us stretched out on top of the sleeping bags as long as we could stand the cold, wearing undershirts and underwear.

"'Whupped'? What the hell is that?"

"You know. 'Wash with soap, Ray, there's still dirt in the cracks of your palms.'"

"Just because she doesn't want him to get hepatitis or something he's whupped. I suppose because I make you use Kleenex instead of your shirt you're whupped too." I wouldn't have admitted it but I felt the same as Henry. We still thought what we had going was so much better than what they had, than what anyone had.

I remember how we whispered then, partly to keep our voices hidden and partly to keep an ear out for the boys' tent, on the other side of the fire. When everyone was asleep we made love, quietly, getting as much in as we could before fire season came and one or the other of us was always away. Henry was happy that night, giggling and making faces until we really got into it. I put my chin on his shoulder and imagined opening myself to the stars, the two of us rutting in the cold fields like a couple of badgers. Alone and free, the offspring turned out to forage for themselves; the male meeting the female at the outer reaches of their separate territories.

A breaking branch makes me jump, but it's just the burned oakbrush settling in on itself. My fingers are starting to get clumsy from the cold and I think that if we could have always been that way—that free—maybe we would have made it. The thought makes me ache with grief and for the first time in four months I wonder what Henry's doing now. If he's out in a Targhee National Forest pickup, trying to get a feel for the new country. Or if he's stuck in a meeting somewhere, his blood pressure ticking up with every minute on the clock. No one there to pass him a goofy note or to jigger his knee; no one there to keep things light.

By the time Ray and I finish dousing the fireline the hillside is socked in. The view has vanished, town and mountains both, so that it's just the two of us, the truck, and the smoldering hillside. The rain's running off my sleeves into my gloves and dripping off my helmet down my neck, and I'm desperately trying to dream up a task to keep me from sitting in that truck with Ray for the next few hours. He's shaking his hose, clearing it of water so it folds better and doesn't mold or freeze; he has an awkward way of doing this, leaning out over his boots and holding the heavy hose at the end of his extended arms. He looks up from it sideways. "Glad to hear you're doing well, over there," he says. Meaning my apartment, I presume, and not where I'm standing as we speak. "It's been a year of change, for sure."

"That it has."

We climb into the front seat to get out of the wet but leave the doors open, our legs slung out the sides. The silence builds up between us.

"Looks like we might have to burn again next week," Ray says. "To get all of it."

I nod.

We get out our lunches. Ray has a sandwich, probably made for him by Rita, that's bulging with fresh produce, and a dinner roll spread with homemade jam. I've got three cheese and cracker packs, slightly crushed. I try not to look envious, although I can already taste the way my mouth will feel after all this salt. On my good days I used to make five sandwiches of a morning, one each for myself and the boys and two for Henry. I'd never been a sandwich person—all that assembly—but I got pretty good at it. I liked standing in the kitchen in the half-dark, putting sandwiches and chips and cut-up carrots into little baggies while the guys stumbled through the shower, one after another.

All that ended after the boys moved to their mother's in Florida. The trailer was deadly silent, like a museum. I'd clean something, straighten the magazines on the table, vacuum the rug, and it would stay just as I'd set it for days. Even Bette and Bruno seemed to tiptoe around. I kept expecting to find Henry crying, or for some little thing to set him off to where we could open up into it, scream, hold each other again, but everything stayed fixed and perfect. I would pat Henry on the shoulder and it was like patting the couch. My total fantasy of married life, Henry to myself and not a single fight, and I could barely breathe.

Ray wipes a mud smear off the dash with his sleeve. "I guess I've never been clear what happened," he says, glancing at me. "That stuff with the boys?" He's nervous, which is what throws me off my guard, I'll decide later. It makes me think I can do this: he's just curious. I think I can handle curious.

I start with the phone call, middle of the night, how the dogs leapt up like they'd been shot. Barking so loud we could hardly think. I'm going to make this good, I decide as I warm into it. Give him his money's worth. I haven't had too many chances to tell this story, and it's great to hear my old voice, hear the way it can tweak and smooth until the mess sounds like just another crazy brouhaha.

"After Henry hung up the phone," I tell Ray, "I remember I yanked on my boots. Didn't even lace them. The light was on, that big fluorescent one in the kitchen, so it was super bright, but to look at us you would've thought it was pitch black. Henry, stumbling around, me, stumbling around, Henry already pissed as a hornet caught in a window. The dogs all crawling around the kitchen floor with their tails between their legs.

"We got to the door and the smoke about knocked us on our *backs*. Little bits of ash floating down like snow."

Ray nods. "You could smell it all the way down in town," he said.

"—I couldn't even tell you if Henry was up ahead of me, or behind me, or what, except that I could hear him yelling"—I make my voice go into a fake growl to imitate him—"*'I'm gonna get you little shits! I'm gonna kill you both!'* And I was like, oh man, better keep *Henry* out of trouble, and I wasn't even thinking about the boys. Like I couldn't grasp it yet or something, how serious it was.

"So there we were, flailing along, coming up on the district fire trucks parked along the road, and we could even see the West Divide fire crew trucks down near the CDOT, and more trucks turning up from the highway—and then we hear this explosion, and I'm like, *oh fuck*. And Bob Brenner gets on the megaphone, and he starts telling everyone to evacuate the area, evacuate the area." I do a pretty good imitation of Bob Brenner's self-important drawl and Ray snickers a little, despite himself.

"And Henry and I pay him absolutely no attention, of course, with Henry on the warpath and me worried that he's going to make some huge fool of himself in front of the entire five-agency fire crew, and then we come up over the ridge."

I pause a moment. I remember the ridge, and how that was the second I realized this was something different than what I thought. I came up over the ridge and saw the heronry in flames, that great forked cottonwood trunk at the center of it burning away like a campfire, and it was like my heart stopped within my chest. The first thing I thought was, the herons. Then, they couldn't possibly have done this. Not the boys. Then I decided it must have been Evan. I could see him doing it, but not Chris. But there they were.

"And that's when we saw the two of them, down by the squad car already." I crumple up my cracker paper and stuff it under the seat. "Half of what the squad car's there for is to protect them from the parents, in that kind of situation. They're not dumb. Because we were livid. Well, Henry was. As the parent. Came screaming down the entire hill in that smoke, it's lucky he didn't keel over with asphyxiation. And I was pretty pissed too by that point."

I wonder how much of this story Ray's heard, and from who. If Officer Davis or any of the West Divide fire crew has told him how I was actually the one to get to the boys first, screaming like some hysterical elephant. I try not to remember this part.

"Not one of my best moments. You know, because this was the thing—they'd taken our fire gear—*these* things. The very propane tank I used today. This very helmet."

Ray shakes his head and says, "You got to wonder what those boys were thinking. Got to wonder."

"Well, not very much, that was clear," I say.

I am remembering how they both looked so tired and worried, their soot-streaked faces lit by the fire. They were wearing my personal protective gear, my helmet and spare helmet, my firefighting jacket and windbreaker. *My* things. I wanted to rip the stuff off their bodies. Evan was practicing an arrogant sneer and Chris was shivering up against him, trying not to cry, and I was having none of it. None of it.

Maybe I kind of did try to tear the clothes off them, because I kept grabbing and snatching at them, screaming, "What about *them*? Did you think about *them*?" Even though it was Evan I finally got ahold of it was Chris I was asking. I had my face down so my nose was almost touching his. "Did you just forget about them just like that? Or do you not even care?" I'm not even sure if they knew I was talking about the herons—well, Evan would have had no idea. But Chris might of, except that he was so scared he was actually trembling. Not even that stopped me, not one whit.

"Not one of my best moments," I repeat again to Ray, shaking my head. My tone's different; I've let the story get away from me. I even feel a weird tremor in my chest, a shaking I'm afraid will spread. I take a deep breath, try to calm myself.

"And you know how the rest of it goes," I add lamely. "The charges, the penalties. What we decided to do, because we had to do something, and then Social Services getting involved. The whole huge mess."

My heart is pounding and I look out the window at the miserable rain, think how for most people it would be the burning that brings back that ash-choked night. For me it's the sodden piss of water on leaves. I'm wishing I'd kept my mouth shut.

Ray clears his throat. He says, "Actually, that was the part I was asking about. How that all happened. Because. Well, because."

I have a sudden image of the trailer on the evening after Henry beat the boys with his Rodeo Days belt. Henry sat in front of the TV with a plate of peas and hot dogs, eyes fixed on the screen but not watching, not responding. I ate my dinner alone at the dining room table. Through the closed door to his room I could actually hear Evan's complete and total scorn; I could also hear the miserable little sobs of Chris. I suppose this was where an intelligent person, a sensitive person, would have done something. But for some reason I thought it would all blow over, that we'd get over it, like we always had. Or else I thought it was already too late. I don't know. That day is kind of a blur, and all I can really conjure up is how the hot dogs felt as big as horse pills going down my throat.

"Henry kept asking me, what should I do, what should I do," I say, hating the way my voice is husky. "I said, I don't know. They're your boys."

Chris those days not even looking at me, not meeting my eye. Sulking, I thought. That was the other thing: all the old roles and alliances were broken. Maybe I was in it just as deep as Henry, only I would never admit it. Have never admitted it.

"Henry'd just keep pestering me. Should we do this, should we do that. Trying out all these ideas, like he was asking for my permission or something." That was how we worked, I want to explain.

I go on. My imitation Henry voice has gotten clumsy, bitter-sounding. *"'On the one hand it was an accident,'* he'd say. *'They were just playing with your fire gear.' 'On the other hand that equipment isn't a toy,'* he'd answer himself. *'And they ought to know that by now. Mistakes have consequences, that's something I've got to teach them. They're just these irresponsible little punks right now. It's goddamn embarrassing.'"*

God, how he was pissing me off. This thing, that thing, what should we do. When all I thought was that it wouldn't matter either way—whatever he did would ignite the blow-up, and then we could wait awhile, and then things would go back to normal. The thing was, I was telling myself all along that it was Henry who had to make the first move. I say, "I just got sick of all Henry's dither dathering. So in the end I was like, go for it."

Ray nods. Thoughtfully. Pretty far cry from your own little home, I want to say, but obviously don't. I want to ask him what he would have done, on the odd chance his honor roll kids went out and torched three snowplows and a wildlife refuge. I want to say, okay, we've had our little heart-to-heart, let's move on.

He brushes some crumbs off his lap, straightens up. "Did you ever find out who told Social Services?" he asks.

It's a question that takes me by surprise. "Well, the boys, we always thought," I say. It wasn't something Henry and I ever talked about. But the boys weren't exactly shy about parading their welts around to any and all who asked, although come to think of it the only ones I knew for sure to have asked them were Social Services, and then later the judge. I remember suddenly how for a while I had a weird suspicion that it was Henry who'd turned himself in, because of the way he just let everything happen after that. He didn't even put up a fight when Darlene, his ex, called collect from Florida to tell him she was going to sue for full custody.

Something in Ray's face changes as he says, "It was a strange time, then. Lee Hale was on leave that month, you remember. So it was just Henry and me down in that basement office. And he was muttering things, muttering and muttering. I never knew what to make of it and then you weren't talking either, wouldn't say nothing to nobody . . ."

"I was trying to stay out of it," I say, my voice a little louder than it needs to be.

"Well, I didn't know what was going on. And it turned out the day I picked to go down and talk to the boys was I guess just the day or so after. After Henry. And when I saw all those bruises and then tried to confront Henry—things just got out of hand."

It's like I know what Ray is trying to say and I don't want to hear it. I lean down and turn on the truck so that we can go somewhere, anywhere, get out of this conversation. I figure we better get down past that tight spot in the road before the roads really get soft and I probably say something like this to Ray. In any case he doesn't seem to have any objection to what we're doing. In fact he's still over there talking, even though I can barely hear him over the noise of the engine and the squeal of the branches taking off our paint.

This is what it sounds like he's saying: "Of course they asked me when I filed the report whether I thought you all posed any danger to the boys. And I don't know. I didn't know what to tell them. So I said I didn't know. Said I didn't think so but I didn't know."

We pull out onto the road and it is greasy. Slick as snot, as we like to say. I'm more cautious than on the way up and I stop to make sure I've got it in four-wheel drive low. No need to rush this, I tell myself, although my toe keeps fluttering the gas a little too hard.

And let me tell you, Ray is not exactly helping. Blabbity blabbity blab. It's like he's had this confession up his sleeve all winter and was just waiting for the perfect moment. "And then when I talked to the boys," he's saying now. "I kept telling myself this. And then when Henry started having his doubts I knew I had to do something."

"Henry had his doubts?" I ask, not even thinking about it. The rain's really coming down and I'm starting to wonder if we shouldn't pull over and wait for the roads to dry out a bit before trying the safety stand down curve. I have a sudden sense of what it will feel like as the wheels lose their grip on the road, as the clutch gives up and we start sliding down.

"You remember how Henry was after that first week. Going around the office telling everyone he didn't think you were fit parents, that maybe once you were but now you weren't. He kept saying, Something has broken, something has broken." I can sense Ray looking at me while he talks, waiting for me to nod in agreement. I can't agree because I don't remember any of this. Henry never said more than two words to me after he hit the boys.

"I knew it," I say. "Henry had a breakdown."

"Nancy, what Henry said is that he'd always thought you kind of loved the boys. In your phone-it-in way. That's how he put it. Phone-it-in way." His rueful laugh makes me jump. "But then after you just didn't do anything, after you just let him—well, he said he didn't know any more. He said it seemed like Evan and Chris could have been any two kids, for all you seemed to care. Whatever he thought the family was built on, he said, was false. And there wasn't any more point to any of it."

Here we are at the curve. I stop the truck. "What?" I say.

"Now I think he might have been over harsh," Ray keeps going, picking at his cuticles nervously. "But at the time, with everything that was going on—well, I wasn't sure. I just wasn't sure."

I open the door before he can lean forward and say anything more in that earnest voice of his. I get out into the rain, saying that I just have to check the road. The rain plasters my hair to my head, my boots thicken with mud, and I see that we couldn't possibly have made it. At least this is what I think I see. It's as if I notice for the first time how incredibly narrow this stretch is, how it seems I could span it with my outstretched arms and I'm sure I couldn't do the same for the truck body. But there is no crumbling, no washout, nothing to show that the road is any different than it's ever been. But it's obvious to me we're going to have to walk out.

I feel light-headed and nauseous, have to lay my hand on the truck's hood to steady myself. Have to lay my forehead on the hood, too, the steaming gritty surface not quite a comfort. I'm furious at my shaking legs. Bad roads are nothing and we're fine, we stopped in time, we'll be able to get out of this just fine. I'm trying not to think about the last time I saw the boys, getting into the truck the morning Henry took them to the airport to send them on their way to Florida. Chris looked so small, the hood of his sweatshirt almost too big for his head. He looked back at the trailer one last time, his face blank and desperate; as he met my eyes I saw his face lift with a sudden something—hopefulness? fear? regret?—and I stepped back from the window, out of his line of sight, as if I hadn't noticed.

Ray opens his door. "You all right?"

I wonder if throwing up would be a satisfactory answer.

"I am not fine, Ray McCallum. I am not fine," I say, finally. I am trying not to think about the things I could have done.

I am trying not to think about what I did not do.

I am trying not to think about the bare apartment I will return to in a few hours, where I will strip off my gear, my sodden jeans and my mud-caked boots, my rain slicker and my rain-soaked shirt and my sweat-soaked bra, with Bette frolicking desperately around my feet. Where I will run the hot water in the shower until the mirror steams up and the great miserable hulk of myself has disappeared and I will not have to look at this great beast breaking down in gusty sobs because the whole great world she had thought she had was gone, forever, gone.

I don't wait for Ray to pull together his things, for him to gather whatever items he thinks are prudent and necessary. I start walking, the mud-caked soles of my boots making a slight sucking sound at each step. By the time I get to the burn line I'm alone, one woman lumbering through the smoldering mess. I don't hear the purr of the truck until it's almost upon me and Ray's leaning out the driver's side window saying, "Get in. Nancy, for God's sake, get in."

ACKNOWLEDGMENTS

VAST THANKS are due to my professors and fellow students at Colorado State University, where many of these stories first appeared in workshop. Huge thanks to the infamous Minions and to my brilliant readers Oz Spies and Cathy Bendl. Also to BK Loren-Cech, for believing in me from the beginning. Thank you to the residencies that generously provided time and space: Playa Summer Lake, Colorado Art Ranch, Kimmel Harding Nelson Center for the Arts, and Hedgebrook. Special thanks to Peggy Lawless and Grant Pound, yak farmers extraordinaire.

Thanks also to the following publications where these stories originally appeared: the *Ontario Review* ("Not a Thing to Comfort You"); the *Laurel Review* ("Gustav and Vera"); *West Branch* ("Bear"); the *MacGuffin* ("Otters"); *New West* ("The Hitchhiker Rule"); *Seed Science Magazine* ("The Four-Foot Moth"); the *Conium Review* ("Endangered Fish of the Colorado River"); the *Masters Review* ("Trespassing"); the *Belmont Story Review* ("Appletree Acres"); and *Nimrod* ("Burning"). To all of the editors who believed in my work and the readers who saw promise in the slush pile: thank you. Thanks especially to Maryse Meijer, Karen Russell, and Carmen Maria Machado.

Finally, none of these stories would have emerged as they did without the love and forbearance of Mike, Silas, and Helen. Thank you.